Promise Me Never

Laikyn Meng

The Orange 9 Publishing Company

18+ Mature content, explicit language, and sexual content. Sensitivity warnings.

THE ORANGE 9 PUBLISHING COMPANY LLC

ISBN: 9798636998358

Contents

To those whose wings have shattered.
To those who found the pieces.
To those who found freedom.
To those that survive the night.
To those who keep trying, always believing in a better
tomorrow.

;

And still, we survive.

<h1 style="text-align:center">Prologue</h1>

RIVER

"**I**'m not going anywhere. I hope you know that. I'm one of those cancers that does not kill you, it just sucks the life out of you." She taps my chest twice and points. I don't think she realizes it, but she does it right over my heart.

The action makes me freeze; we both agreed, decided that there wouldn't be an us. Couldn't be, it wasn't an option. Not after what happened to Sawyer.

We agreed on never; she believes she will drown in consequences before we can reach a happily ever after.

Zailey said it to me like I had told it to her a thousand times. But her voice didn't shake as she glared up at me, so close in our embrace. She didn't know what I'd done, how I was at fault but blamed her.

We were ruined for the rest of our lives. In comparison, our attraction and even interaction wouldn't be dwindled by the climax of an artificial high.

It wasn't as easy as true love; it was a destined clash of want and need. We were both trying to feed a dirty hunger that was never fulfilled. Only the other having the source to keep us satisfied.

"Promise me, River. Promise me that we won't ever be victims again, especially to those who have more control than care. Promise me, River, or we'll be the ones that are buried under a willow tree at the edge of town." Black muddy tears scrawled down her narrow cheeks like they were the depth of veins, dark and destructive.

"I...I can't, Zailey..." Choked up with my own remorse and stabbing guilt for wanting her while my first love was a plague between us.

"Promise me never?" She needed this, I reminded myself. Z was sharp, but she wanted to know we were on the same side.

A side I recognized as the right side for the wrong reasons. Desperate to prove this fate, I wanted the sun to start striking. Placing people back in their places, where the heavens were obedient, and my life wasn't threatened by words and watching eyes.

"I promise." Because at 18, it was the only vow I wanted to be burned at the stake to protect.

Chapter 1

RIVER

Being inside her body was not a sensation I have ever felt before. Sex was uncomplicated. It was the same ecstasy that got the edge off. But the way her body ignited with mine, so in sync that I felt the moments actually slow.

Sex with Sawyer hadn't been this way. Didn't feel this electric; it was a warm body against mine. Zailey's was a magnet, making opposites attract and blend together.

One hand bringing her face closer to mine, our eyes meet, and tears are gripping the edges. A deep connection builds our bond, and I move with every cell I sense. Hers match the same rhythm. We take off, never fully coming down. Even after the high, trying to catch our damn breaths like fresh air would compare.

"Sawyer, that was—"

"Sawyer?" I recognize the voice as something else, someone besides the name I called. Too familiar that I left a mishap.

"Oh shit! No, fuck, I forgot."

Zailey runs around the room, picking up a black thong and lace bra.

"You forgot that my best friend, your girlfriend, wasn't me?"

"Ex, she's my ex-girlfriend." I run my hands through my hair. Leaning up against the headboard as she rushes to get away from the flames.

"Chill, Zailey. It was a mistake."

Deer in the headlights as I say the word mistake. Her head snaps, and I curse another explicit one.

"It's not what I meant, damn woman. Could you just sit down? We need to talk about this." I ask her to stay, but I'm not eager enough to make her.

"Talk about what, River? How I've been pining after you before Sawyer claimed you as hers? God, this is ridiculous! What is wrong with me? You never saw me when she was around and now that she's gone..."

"Will you stop already? What, you think because she is dead is the only reason we fucked? It would have happened eventually."

"Of course, it would have because I'm just a slut who sleeps with my friend's boyfriend."

"Ex-boyfriend." My reflexes must be playing catch up because her shoe smacks me right in the forehead.

"You're never gonna see me, are you, darlin'? It will always be her."

"Jealousy doesn't look good on you, Z."

"It isn't jealousy, it's the rage I can't contain. I've been taking it out on the wrong people."

"What's that supposed to mean?"

But she doesn't answer; her eyes say a goodbye that makes fear a real factor in my life.

"Z! Zailey? What the fuck does that mean?" But when I open the door, she's gone, and my brothers are fighting, so I can't get through. Call out her name one more time, make a sound escape where we both worry about suffocating.

Our momma preaches to us about what love is. Her favorite scripture was inscribed into most of the walls in every room of our house growing up.

She taught us love was patient, that love was not self-seeking. But the young lady I fell on my face for wasn't patient, rarely kind, but she has always been mine.

Though I knew one phrase in that speech that stuck with me most: *"It always protects, always trusts, always hopes, and always perseveres."*

Zailey wasn't my first pick; I would probably regret that decision the rest of my life. She definitely commanded attention, and I saw the fluctuation trying to compete with her best friend. At the time of 17, I was cocky, and damn, I am still a good looking son of a bitch. Back then I wanted someone who was on top, not scared off by stepping into the spotlight, leaving her friends in the shadows.

Her name is my favorite word. The sound of her sighing after a nightmare is my favorite sound. The same one when the rain stops and lightning returns to her soul. My ideal sense knows you would be okay without me, that you don't need me, but that you would choose me.

Chapter 2

ZAILEY

Her funeral started 20 minutes ago, and I even debated going inside. Once her body was buried in the ground, I knew I could breathe.

The clock ticks and reminds me as every second passes, down the road in a church filled with people I've known my entire life, mourning.

My mother is in her bedroom, my brother playing video games. Besides that noise, there is nothing. At the table, I sit alone as I stare out the kitchen window waiting for Calvary to burn me alive.

They probably are playing her favorite songs, her cousins singing sweet words with tears falling from their eyes.

Her parents huddled together, whispering love. The Hendrix clan taking up a few rows with their burly bodies. River, yes, River would be there. Front row probably, not listening to the speakers. He stares at her closed coffin, wishing it was me.

Yes, River Hendrix wouldn't be smiling ear to ear or crying uncontrollably. He was calculated; he showed little emotion unless he knew it would serve him a purpose, gain his momentum.

"Zailey?" My brother Indie calls for me.

"Yeah?"

"Is Mom going to get better? Or is she going to die?" His fingers still click around on his controller.

"It's nothing you need to worry about, buddy."

"Will we go live with Dad after she dies? Or will we stay here with JuJu?"

"Do you like staying with Dad?" I contemplate what would actually happen to us. Would my father come to collect us, or would we stay with my mother's friend?

"Yes, I think spending weekends with him is fun. I know you don't usually go. But Dad and I do lots of activities and watch movies together. He even allows me to cook on the stove with him."

Truth is, our dad was a good guy who did the best he could. Sad news that our mother's health was declining, I think we both felt it. She would be gone sooner than we had time to process it.

What would I do? Move to his house? I got my GED last month. Thought it would be handy if I ran away. The letters were out there, and minds were processing a new loss for their lost soul.

Lying next to her as I heard her choke her last breath, those minutes were an eternity. Though my head was bleeding and my shoulder seemed to be numb down to my wrist. I didn't scream out for help. I didn't holler in pain.

Closed my eyes and I counted. I tried to relax through the pain she caused me for years. Pretending it was normal when it felt wrong.

I tried not to feel horrible about what I had done. Before the car incident, I wrote a letter to her parents. It explained all the things Sawyer showed me. The same message went to my father's office, two towns over. My mother was the last one to read it. But, I made sure that I was going to be the one that needed to end things before it blew up.

Dying makes you a hero. No matter the secret crimes you've committed. You become glorified, stone etched with only the blood of innocence. A few days after, her mother came over, screeching up a storm. Calling me a liar, pointing a finger. She was so angry she threw my brother's pet rocks at our windows, one missing my head.

Sawyer's dad shook his head, disappointed and disgusted. I rounded the house to get the hose, hoping to spray away the debris. River was there, lurking to see if I was, in fact, the fraud I'd been accused of being.

The heat I got from them wasn't as brutal as the way he cursed me. "Why would you make something like that up about at Sawyer, your best friend? She would have done anything for you, she always did. Were you jealous? She always said that you wanted me. Huh, Zailey? Were you too wounded to know you wouldn't win me? I loved her, only her. I never once looked at you the way I saw her."

I didn't say anything. I bit down on my lip and stared at the ground, wondering if it was true. Maybe I was a liar, perhaps I deserved the cruel experiments, the intrusion into my young body. Perhaps it was all I was suitable for, being an object to receive the suppression she couldn't explain.

"It sucks, I feel so sorry for you. Sawyer was the spotlight, and you couldn't bear her having something you wanted." He cocked his head back and leaned forward, spitting at my feet; it might as well have been my face.

"Well, are you going to say anything, darlin'? Or have you gotten all of your crazy out of your system? Bet you are regretting your confession now. She's dead, Zailey, and you can never apologize. That is something you have to live with the rest of your miserable life."

At 16, I never once had a *fuck you* attitude. I'd been polite, been obedient. But right here, this is what made me snap. In the cruelest of ways, I brought a smile up to my face.

"Does it scare you that you didn't have the faintest idea of who your perfect girlfriend really was?"

"You don't know her like I do, well, did. Thanks to you."

"I didn't drive us off a cliff, that was your beloved's choice. But, you want to know something I have that you don't?"

"What?"

"Her last words, those moments before impact. I feel bad you never got to meet the monster side of Sawyer."

"And I'm sorry you weren't getting enough attention that you had to concoct some fabrication to make you feel more valid. Tell you one thing, girl, my dick had a nice time stealing that innocence between your legs."

The slap was intentional. I'd forecasted this fight for weeks. Finally, the showdown was a relief.

"I bet I can tell you the only way she got off was by hurting you, on the pressure point near your pelvis or the one on the side of your neck."

Barely his eyes grew with shock.

"We all have our kinks."

"River, honey, I'm sorry you are mourning your girlfriend you had for six months. Happy anniversary, by the way. But, I've known that girl since we were kids. We were each other's first kisses, and I was her last." Amen.

Chapter 3

RIVER

There was no way the stuff Zailey mocked up in that note could be right, utter bullshit to the bone. Sawyer was my first love, and I couldn't bear it for her to be blackmailed with a bad rep.

"Give me another, brother." We sat around the dining room table. Each of my brothers and their significant others by their sides. Ranger, Richter, Ryotte, Razer. Except for my three youngest brothers Rhode and the twins; Ryder and Rayce who were still mingle and of course we tended to mingle.

My dad, Rusty, sat on the end of the couch while he massaged my mother's feet. The long slab of wood held many memories, meals, birthdays; it was the first place I held Sawyer in my arms and told her she was mine.

She laughed and grabbed my face, smacking the biggest kiss with a tangled tongue I ever got in my life.

"Dude?" Ryder holds a beer bottle out to me, and I take it, draining it within 30 seconds.

"Want something stronger?" Razer holds up the bottle of whiskey and I give him a nod.

"Watch yourselves, gentlemen, I won't be cleaning up your puke." The sweet taunt from our mother's voice carries through our log cabin.

"Careful, Raze, last time, River outdrank you. Wouldn't want your baby brother to knock your ego any further." Ryotte pours himself a shot, before winking at our brother.

"The first one to upchuck gets dish duty for a month." Rhode settles his shot glass next to the others.

"I can't believe your mom lets you guys drink. My parents would have whooped my ass if they caught me around such bad influences." Richter's girlfriend shakes her head, disbelieving all before her.

"Darling, the difference between your parents restricting you and me allowing them is that at our house at least I know they aren't hiding anything, and the most important—"

"We're all safe." The chorus of boys sings the last phrase she repeatedly told us growing up.

"Well, I um, have an announcement before all of you get shitfaced and don't remember our last name." Rayce stands up, and he smiles a shy look as he tries to get his speech out.

"Awe, little Rayce has put on his big boy pants." Ryotte gets an elbow to the gut by the spitfire of his wife.

"Shut your trap, or you are going to sleep in the shed."

"Spit it out, boy." Our father whistles from his position. His voice means business, and his eyes look down on his youngest son, already sensitive to the dread of what is to come.

We all shut up and focus on Rayce. Tension in the air rises high. It might be from the alcohol floating in our blood. But I feel it.

"Well, you've got your stage; let us hear your declaration." My mother stares at my father with a pinched face. Why is he such a dick?

The man was intimidating; we all outgrew him in height, but no one could reach his level of anger.

"I—I've wanted to—to come out and talk to all of you for a while now." Ryder sits next to him, staring at the table, taking another swig of his drink.

"Now, you're stuttering? Can't you speak without acting like a child?" The cookbook in mom's hands smacks the side of her husband's head.

Rayce visibly tries to take a step back but is in between the chairs. He doesn't look at us for comfort; we sit amongst the discomfort.

Some of the girls try to speak up against him; that never ends well.

"Rusty, why don't you find your manners or your ass will have a new hole." The only response he gives is rubbing his forehead where the book smacked.

"Go on, honey." Too sweet to be sour, she would die for sons even at the hands of our father.

"I'm gay, Mom." Rayce's head hangs in shame, and the room goes silent. We look at her; she doesn't seem surprised.

Her smile is kind, and she nods, accepting him fully.

Before we can interfere, our dad has Rayce slammed against the wall, his forearm against his throat.

"What the fuck did you say?" We feel the spit from here.

"Dad!"

"LET HIM GO!"

"OH MY GOD!"

Screams give way among the shouts. We are holding each other back. Trying to get to our father.

"Now I may be getting older, but I swear my hearing must be tricking me. There couldn't be in any world, especially this one, where a son of mine, blood from my blood, could be a fucking homo." Rayce's eyes are vast, and he was struggling to breathe. The fear of man wiping out his courage.

Ranger grabbed my dad around the neck, holding him in a headlock.

"You aren't going to suffocate him for being gay, release him." His voice was the strictest out of us all.

"Step back, Rang." To the side of us, Rowan Hendrix holds a shotgun up to our father. "If you do not let go of my son, the boys will be visiting their mother behind bars."

"Mom! What the fuck are you doing?" Rhode is pulling out his hair; Ryder remains seated.

Richter tries to take the gun, but he backs away when my mom aims it at him.

"Now, Rusty." Our momma doesn't even break a sweat threatening the old man.

He puts his hands up, shrugs my brother's grip off of him. Walks backward as he spits, "I'd rather you be dead than be a flaming faggot. Ryder told me he caught some guy sucking you off. Best you go find yourself a new place to live, boy; your kind ain't welcome here." Busting through the front door.

It wasn't the first time our father was faced with a challenge with the way he was raised. Some of my brothers' lovers were minorities, an adjustment that took him a few months to understand.

"Rayce, you okay?" I go up to check as he crumples to the floor. He coughs and wheezes, puts his head down on his knees.

"Fuck, girls, would you excuse us for a moment?" The wives and girlfriends flee to the back bedrooms, free to escape the brutality.

"Mom, you weren't really going to shoot him, were you?" Rhode's concern is misplaced, and we all give him a look.

"Don't give it another thought, Rhode. Wasn't the first time I had to pull a gun on your father."

"Rayce, you good, man?"

"Just leave me alone, get away from me." He staggers to get up but rushes out the side door before we can stop him.

"Whoa, man," Ryotte calls after him, but we give him a minute to cool down.

Our mother makes her way over to the table. She sits across from Ryder who can't look her in the eyes.

She places the shotgun between them.

"Is there a good reason I shouldn't smack you over the head for selling out your brother to make your sins look less grand?" Her breath tries to catch up with posture.

We all try to calm the nerves raging, getting everyone antsy.

"Dad will get over it. He's the perfect child, besides Rhode. Why does it matter? So he has one flaw to point out? No reason to hate the guy." His knuckles start tapping underneath the wood.

"Well, you've hit one."

This time, his brown eyes meet her dark realms, and I would beg for mercy at this point. Being on the other end of her rampage doesn't end well for anyone.

"Son of a bitch." One of my brothers calls out.

"How are you going to make this right, Ryder?"

"Make what right? I can't take it back." The little bastard has the balls to shrug, and I swear there is a twitch in my mom's jaw. She holds back, wanting to give him a good whack over the head.

"Listen to me, and you better listen damn good, you little shithead. If you hadn't explicitly outed your brother, which by the way, is not your business one fucking bit, McKenzie Kershaw, that girl who committed suicide because of something you and your dumbass buddies all played a part in, would still be dead, Ryder. It doesn't help that Rayce found her and tried to take the fall for you." Cutthroat.

"Mom." Razer calls out to her, but she puts a hand up, telling him to stay the fuck out of it before his secrets get spilled.

"Does it make you feel better? To know you took away his brave moment because you felt inferior? Tell me, Ryder, did your sins wash away the minute you decided to share the gossip?" Her eyes level him, and we all stand, holding our breaths waiting.

"If you can only be loyal to yourself, you weren't paying attention to being raised right. Rayce is your brother, your twin, for god's sake. It wasn't the wolves you threw him to, it was an unforgiving devil."

She stands up and stretches, smooths out her apron and dress.

"Boys, why don't you pick your jaws off the floor and go do something useful. Lunch needs to be prepared; run along to your women. I'm sure they were all scared half to death by your father's episode. One more thing, Ryder, get the hell out of my house. And someone for the love of God, go get Rayce and bring him back here."

Momma ain't too keen on betrayal. Love was her motto in every sense of the word. She lived by that commandment. Forcing one son out to give a place for another a safe haven, well, I bet her heart was skipping beats from the vows she was breaking.

"Man, she hasn't called in two months. I'm worried maybe something is wrong, I heard her mom hasn't been doing well."

"Who?" My hands and eyes are busy with the video game in front of us.

"Z." It's Rhode's voice from the corner of our living room with a book in his hands.

"Fuck her." Razer is right there to back me up.

"Don't be an ass." Rayce strolls in and flops down, grabbing a controller.

I haven't moved since I severed our ties. Our hands suddenly wild with whirlwinds and range. But I stayed isolated and smoked the right amount of my inheritance in weed and drank even more in alcohol.

My curtains stained with regret and sorrow.

"Should we go out?" Ryder asks.

We all answer no.

"Want to get laid? Maybe it will help you blow off some steam."

"No." My word final.

"When was the last time you jerked off?" Razer is an avid believer in making yourself feel the best.

"Can't get it up." I shrug my shoulders, still not looking anywhere but the screen.

"What?" The room falls silent.

"No use." I pull another bottle and find a lighter. The sticker faded with a purple star, decorated by Zailey.

"How much longer do you need?" To mourn, to forget, to heal.

"Three months tops; give me one more month, and I'll be good as new." By then, I would be starting college. I would be out of this town where her name stained the one that fell from my lips.

"I never want to see you again." It was the softest betrayal, leaning in, almost kissing the stray hairs. But I took that away.

"I'm not lying, I wouldn't do such a thing. River, you know I wouldn't. Please, if there is any doubt in your bones, any at all. You know it might be impossible to believe, but it's true."

She is breaking down, and I have nothing but the sheer decency to look the other way, hoping she stops the pained theatrics.

"There is nothing left to say, Zailey." Not allowing even a shred of wonder take its place inside my mind.

There isn't a possibility where this could be true. But girls like her always needed to prove the impossible.

My smile was light, and it permitted me the pleasure of allowing myself at least that much time to grieve. Because after that 3rd-month mark, there was no going back to what could have been. All possibilities are burning in the front lawn with her memory.

~

Chapter 4

ZAILEY

Olallie nudges me to go outside. We watch the new girl get dropped at the curb by her parents.

"O, if you want to go welcome her, that is all on you, sparkle. But, since you've known me a couple months, we will have to both agree I am not on that committee." We continue to stare at the edge where freedom ends.

I get two taps on the shoulder before I roll my eyes and move to the door.

"You owe me, Olallie girl." The obedient girl follows behind me. A 14-year-old with the same ammunition to harbor exoneration.

A new brown-haired girl lies on the warm cement like she is taking a vacation from life. With a newly lit joint between her lips, maybe breath is taking a leave of absence for her.

"Hey, chick? You wanna share your stash, or you going to be a selfish bitch?" She cocks her head to look at my statement hair first and tries to decide if I'm worth the time.

The typical response when you got white, blue, purple streaked throughout my roots.

"Are you new here? Sorry to disappoint you, but there's no grand welcome wagon." The puckered bitch face more on point than ever before.

"Say please, Stormy." I guess she didn't come here to make friends. Maybe I should take up the same mission statement.

Olallie starts to giggle and starts wiggling her fingers around like some crazed person, delighted with my pain.

"Yo, O! That is an insult! It isn't funny." She tries to explain something, but damn, I don't have it in me to fight it.

"Yeah, you are right. I have been called worst. Fuck, I need to learn some manners. This chick is Olallie, she's deaf. I'm Zailey, not stormy. I'm here in this safe haven because my father told me I was inclined to self-destruct. And you are?" My scrubs itch me with their scent of bleach. Lucky Olallie gets to wear her usual attire; maybe it's from having a daddy who holds power.

"Harper." The name fits her like the Spanish flu finding a host.

"What's with the brace?"

"Car accident."

"Gnarly." Harper hands me a cigarette, and I take it, hopefully able to hide it for later. She offers one to O, but she shakes her hair.

I know what's coming, the inevitable Olallie shakedown of your soul. Stripped bare of natural defense tendencies.

"Well, welcome to our home."

"Never felt more accepted than I do right now. Should we save our group hug for later?"

"Listen, bitch, I think you might fit in here. Olallie, do not get all friendly with her. She likes everybody, and I mean everybody, so don't go thinking you are special or anything. Olallie has a sixth sense of knowing people's truths. If I were you, I would steer clear of bluebonnet here, or she will try and heal you." I flip my hair and head back towards the entrance.

Poor girl probably gets stuck with one of the frantic freaks like Anika.

We all sit around in group therapy, reading all the others share, including the new girl who wants to slam Ryder back his shit.

"Zailey, you haven't shared once since you've been here."

"What? That can't be possible! And here, each page of my journal is filled with hopeful antidotes to ease our heavy minds. Oh, shit, I'm sorry, no, I've got stick figure doodles, and damn is that a cornucopia of my favorite desserts. Guess we are out of luck."

No words were ever going to end up on those jailbird pages. I turned my nose up at the mere thought of spilling my guts to a therapist who told flashed PTSD side effects at me like a wiz kid with flashcards.

Poor therapist needs to relearn how to relate to others. Each time he opens his mouth, I find myself wondering if sawyer would be here instead of me. Would her name be on a roll call at breakfast in the morning?

If I was dead, would she be the one punished for living through her attempt to make us end?

Maybe Sawyer and River would kiss in new sunsets. On plains untouched by the rocky mountains.

One thing I knew for sure was this wasn't a fairytale. I wasn't going to be saved, and I knew the better part of me didn't want to be.

The night Sawyer tried to finish us, by driving off a cliff, made me crack wide open. Her plea for intimacy became uncomfortable to be near. A closet lesbian too scared to accept that I wasn't her soul mate. But her boyfriend had always been mine. And if she couldn't have me, nobody could. Not even myself. It was a curse she promised as she leaned in to kiss me one last time. Just before I jolted back, and her neck snapped with the impact of the tree line below us.

She made one mistake through our descent. I'd been preparing to die for as long as my mother had. The fear of death rippled through her pores, and she looked to me for comfort. But I didn't have any; my only regret is that I didn't kiss her goodbye. Because in that kiss, she would have realized it was only a matter of time before we all perished.

Last Halloween, I was dancing in your arms. We were joking while grinding on each other, trying to make your significant other jealous. But she didn't rise quickly. If I am honest, I was getting carried away. The lady boner was invisibly stabbing every party goer that walked within a 5-foot radius of me. Equating into wet panties all night, or moist lips give or take. Because there was a lack of cloth between my thighs.

After a while, we lost ourselves in the act and then in each other. Sawyer didn't move, and some part of her stare made it uncomfortably clear she didn't mind. I almost brought your chin down toward me so I could kiss your lips. Finally, the temptation would be sedated.

It was me who pointed you out at our high school rivals assembly. I should have realized then our friendship was disfigured. Because the way Sawyer smiled at me, not even acknowledging who you were, it's like she wanted to steal the one thing I wanted. Because the truth was, there were no boy crushes and no brushes of secrets until it came to you.

A year and a half of trying to reign in the jealousy, even the night I sat with my ear next to the wall as you took her virginity, and she made sure I would remember the range of her moans.

She didn't claim you; you chose her. There wasn't a competition when Sawyer came into play; all eyes were on her, and I drifted to the sidelines where the spotlight never hit me.

This year, I am stuck behind locked doors, keys held by nursing staff, and supervised clinicians. I don't wear a slutty costume to get your attention. I don't call you to tell you I've made a mistake, we could try and salvage ourselves.

But then I stop and I wonder. I think maybe too much damage from the past could never heal our present. Too many factors leading you down the path of resentment and me to second best.

One thing I know for sure is Sawyer can't reach me while I am grieving her lover.

I slept with one of your brothers; had it been an option. I would have slept with more. Out of hate, and revenge, out of the sadness of never ending up like her. I met Olallie and became best friends with Harper Calico in this place. Calico also fell victim to your brother; weak girls always do.

He likes to take advantage of his own insecurities when he sees them glorified in the opposite sex. It makes him feel the power, gives him strength because, in the back of his mind, he dwells on the thought. At least I am not that weak or pathetic.

"It started after the funeral, my mother's, not Sawyers." I pinch my sides, trying to calm the waves of discomfort I feel releasing this information a stranger.

Dr. Candy did a coy once-over, stopping at my hair before I continued with my speech.

"We went to live with my father two towns over. Indie, my little brother he's twelve years old. Dad never got re-married; they had a lot of one on one time together." A smile grows on my face, seeing my little brother's eyes light up with the father and son time.

She looks out the window, lost on her own dime. It helps me calm down. Maybe she is pretending, or perhaps she isn't paying attention at all. Both thoughts help me relax even further into the chair, like curling up for a good movie.

"One day, I was out on the job with my dad; he owns an electric company. Last few weeks, I got into trouble with a couple guys. He was installing a new theater system for a home that was getting built. At first, it was an accident. I bumped a small charged wire. It scared me, but then it felt different, almost pleasant."

I rub my fingers together, remembering the friction of a spark that radiated through my skin. The temptation fades after I blink, seeing the confusion in my dad's eyes.

"He never brought up the letter. I saw it open on his dresser after we moved. I stopped and stared at it; when he came up he took it and tucked it away in a drawer. It made it easier, you know."

"What did?" Aw, and our loyal therapist responds.

"Ignoring what happened to me didn't happen."

"But, it did, Zailey." Her glasses pushed up her face, and she looks elegant and beautiful. Someone my mother would have loved to persuade her daughter.

"Yes, but it shouldn't have. Sometimes, I wonder if I was too weak to walk away. Sawyer didn't chain me to a wall in her closet. Wasn't locked in a basement with no escape. Why didn't I ever say anything before I sent those letters, before that night when she drove us off a cliff?"

"Being assaulted traumatizes a person; a sense of Stockholm syndrome could have been in effect."

"Could have been, what kind of diagnosis is that Dr. Candy?"

"I'm a little off my game today, Zailey. If you want, I can get another therapist on duty to take over." She sighs and looks down at the floor, ashamed.

"No, if you don't mind, it's nice just to say it out loud. It doesn't really matter if you listen or not."

She nods and sits back.

"There's this scar that travels up my torso around the side of my belly button. It was too long, and I couldn't pull the current away. It was the worst time, might as well have been around my throat the way it scared the shit out him. He thought I had fried myself up like chicken on the southern plains."

We gave small infractions of a laugh.

"He didn't know what to do with me. Honestly, I can't blame him. It's better this way; they're better just the two of them. I fit in here, with a roommate who can't hear me have panic attacks at night. My friends are two twin boys whose brother made it apparent I should update my status to irrelevant. Lastly, one girl, who doesn't seem remotely awful won't speak two words to me." Olallie has been a haven; sometimes I'll come out of a nightmare, and she is there grazing her fingers over my forehead, calming my mind's eye.

"The place does not seem to be making you worse by any degrees. If you want my opinion, you could be in jail, not getting help. Here you have a chance to reconcile the past and choose a different future." Wise ol' Candy returns to the session.

"Is your name really Dr. Candy?"

"Candice."

"Don't have a last name you appreciate?"

"It's a negative synonym for the kind of work I do. Best not to remind people of the drug they love to use on themselves." She closes her folder, a pen gently tucked inside.

"I enjoy a good guessing game! Let me see, a drug that people use that is harmful. Weed? Beers? Hash? Candy Stash?" I stand, straightening out the sweatshirt as she unlocks the door.

With one look over the shoulder, she looks at me with understanding. "Payne, Zailey. Your favorite drug is pain. Just happens to be the same as my last name."

Chapter 5

ZAILEY

"Why does it seem like Zailey Jensen is acting like she doesn't know who we are, Rayce?" Ryder Hendrix saunters up with his swag, his twin following behind him.

These boys are familiar to me, one more intimately than I would like to admit. While the other glances over me without interest. A distaste that confirms my own feelings for myself.

I continue to stare at the seats where Olallie chats with the new girl, Harper or Calico. She came in nonchalant brooding, tried to put Ryder in his place.

Too bad that boy doesn't give a damn.

"Aw, the new treat is feisty, isn't she? Can't wait to break her in for a good ride. Got to use my tender touch, though, seems like the beauty has a small gimp." Ryder rubs his jaw, with a cocked smile, so sure of the unattainable.

"Ry, take it easy." Rayce lifts two fingers at his brother's comment. I try not to engage. I hesitate to even participate in the defense.

It won't end well for me.

They are a reminder of punishments that won't be met with lessened time for good behavior.

"Ryder, I'm surprised your dick hasn't fallen off with you sleeping with half the state." My hands hang over the back of the chair, keeping my bitch face evident.

"If I am correct, you are included in that statement. Are you slut-shaming yourself now, darlin'? My what would River think of our sexcapade?" His light green eyes twinkle at the enticement.

"Rayce, did he choose to come here because he knows you have a bigger cock than him? Always second best, aye there, buddy?" I stand, knocking over the chair as I head back to my room.

Facing my demons is a brutal bastard that makes my head spin.

Breathe, don't let them get to you. Count to 5 or 3,000; do not lose your cool again.

It isn't what you think, or maybe it is. "River." His name makes me back into a corner and recoil. The look on his face, the final once-over as he shakes his head and spits at my feet.

"It wasn't my fault, she wouldn't listen." My hot palms cover my ears, hoping the screams will fade into permanent silence.

Olallie is blessed with a glorious gift. My signing roommate, who ripped out her hearing implants like she was exchanging earrings with outfits.

Her tolerance for pain made all the girls here weak ass crybabies. The chick was indeed more messed up than any other melodramatic soul in this place.

"No. No, no, no." A tremor breaks through my body, and I am out of control, trying to tame the attack.

"Please!" I beg to the echo of my voice. My fingers lose feeling as they shake. Something takes over me, and I can't see, but I don't dare blink.

When those eyelids fall, I see her smiling face so bright and happy it makes me sick.

"Leave me alone!" I start to chant. *Leave me alone...*

But Sawyer never does, and her laugh mocks me further into a coma of torture. This time, River comes to join the dismantling of my power.

Yet, he isn't the one that mocks me with ill intent. No, my own personal poltergeist has claimed a title of genuine loyalty.

"Zailey?" Dr. Candy tries to pull me out of the dark hole I've been buried in, but only tears fall instead of the secrets she was hoping.

But I couldn't face her. I couldn't face anyone with the embarrassment of being a 12-year-old girl. Not fully understanding that what was happening between friends wasn't okay.

"Sawyer said she saw it in a show her dad use to watch."

"Saw what?"

"These two girls touching each other." Candy wanted to dish about the encounter; there were many after the first one.

"Zailey? Can you describe your first sexual encounter?"

At first, my eyes flame with anger. I shake my head, not because I couldn't, but because I didn't want to tell her.

Nobody would know the shame of being taken advantage of, the critical adjustment between being understood and being scolded.

"I—I can't talk about it…Sawyer didn't mean any harm, she was just showing me…" In her death, I still defend her.

My best friend for years, scarring my soul in more ways than visible.

"You trusted her, believed she would do no wrong."

"She couldn't have known…" But she probably did. Maybe it happened to her, perhaps I should have asked.

"Zailey…how long did it go on?"

"Go on?" There isn't a specific time or date. I remember seeing River line up as they announced the football players on the opposing team.

His grin was full; his broad shoulders were even more expansive. River laughed, and it struck me in the chest. I couldn't hear it from so far away, but damn if I felt the rumble.

Those eyes snagged on something near me, then refocused as they found me. We were met with the same flash that he blinked twice but held my glare.

"What are you looking at?" Sawyer whispered in my ear; my skin grew bumps as barriers.

When I don't respond, she locks on what the object that holds my attention. She waves, and all captivation River had on me now resides only on her.

I can remember the transition into becoming a 3rd wheel; it must have been at that moment.

Sawyer wouldn't let me have anything that didn't belong to her. My attention, a guy, my own body.

"I'm so sorry...I shouldn't be this weak anymore." Weak, no one called me that, just myself.

"Zailey, you aren't weak," Candy whispered, but I was on a roll, and she wanted to know.

I wanted to be freed of the burden of blaming a victim.

"Seventh grade, we got permission to spend the night at her house without her parents home." Every day, I pray the memories will go away; slowly, I will get to a point in my life where I won't be haunted by her.

But I know it won't be easy, memories are fickle. They rearrange, they mislead, and sometimes, they grow over all the happy childhood ones.

"We were in her bedroom, Sawyer started taking off her clothes, and she wanted me to do the same…"

Sawyer was a stuck-up blonde bitch, one that threw curses in my defense. She was a crazed hormonal cheerleader who was obsessed with River Hendrix, and before I knew it, me.

We were best friends, but there was evidence that she always was trying for more. I was progressive; I flirted when her eyes were hungry, trying to keep her entertained. But I wanted River, man oh man, did I ever want a guy before.

She kept her legs locked around his hips while I sat in the living room, listening to their whispers.

What kind of fucked up friendship was that? Not that I attempted to steal him away from her, but he didn't need her making him jealous and playing games with his beautiful mind.

How I lusted for his hands to squeeze my breasts, have his fingers find pleasure darkness between my thighs.

When our clouds of smoke intertwined, it felt like our fingers were holding onto forever.

Chapter 6

RIVER

As I headed over to the kitchen, I check over to where Amos is hanging around Preacher. Dude has always been bad news. He's been slipping Amos pills behind my back.

Fuck, I'm not his mom or anything, but the guy is spiraling out like he signed up to be the test dummy in an explosion.

Both of us seemed haunted by past encounters. I was doing my best to be there for Amos, give a shoulder to lean against. My own were weighed down with a severity I couldn't face.

Failure wasn't a word I slapped over my forehead. Our father used the term in defining degrees on my little brother, Rayce, a time or two.

It came to that once before, when he found out that one of his sons didn't sail the same way as the rest of us. Well, he sure let his feelings known.

We were divided after that; some of my brothers sided with him. Our mother caught in the middle, trying a ceasefire. But we were all getting burned, especially her and Rayce.

Someone hands me a shot, and I shoot it down without another thought. I stop looking over my shoulder when I see Amos leave with a girl.

The worries fade; the mission to keep everybody else afloat makes me wash away the pain that lurks on the sidelines. Blinding me with grief, giving me motion sickness with the whiplash of regret.

"River! You want in on the next one?" A game of beer pong started, and guys from our football team all waved me over. I took another shot, knowing I could block out the noise, black out the images. Maybe forget the faces of girls I once thought I loved and loved me back.

"Yeah, I'm in..." Each step was intentional, and I realized that no one was looking out for me. After taking care of others, I wasn't about to be burdened with trying to figure my shit out anytime soon.

Chapter 7

ZAILEY

When I wake up the next morning, I tell myself this is different. Today will be a new way to either destroy or heal myself.

Olallie left a couple weeks ago, Harper a few more after her. Here we are, empty brigade. Three days, three days, and then I will be reunited with the intoxication of the real world.

River's brothers still linger the compound like we are meant to be the last ones standing.

Rayce stands next to the art stand, while Ryder argues with the nurse for an extra pill to calm his hysteria.

"Why don't you like me, youngest Hendrix brother?"

"Stop fucking my brothers." He doesn't even have the glee of the insult to give me a look.

He has balls, I'll give him that.

"What about messing with you?" I line up to the stand next to him.

"Stick your hand on my cock. If you get it hard, by all means, jump on for a rodeo." He grabs his junk, jostling it about to make his point.

"You don't think I can get you up?" Teasing him more, trying to avoid the question.

"I know for a damn fact you can't make this cock, probably the biggest one you've ever seen, turn into a steel pipe." He takes the paintbrush and chucks it to the ground.

"Not good enough for you? Been passed around by too many brothers?"

Rayce shakes his head, swaying it back and forth with flare.

"Damn, you are something else."

When he still doesn't look at me, I tilt my head until I get his full attention. The only thing that comes out is an exaggerated sigh, a good eye roll worth.

"I hope you are going to clean up after yourself, Rayce." The aid that Harper connected with walks around us, before leaving us to the mess.

"Whatever you say, Rae." Rayce clicks his tongue as he watches her leave. His eyes go to his brother, already bored with his tantrum.

"Ryder, when's the last time I fucked a vagina?" This gets Ryder to stop his meltdown and look over at us, perking up at the dirty banter.

"Rayce, language!" Dr. Candy screams at us as she walks Anika into her office.

"Dude hasn't stuck his wiener in a girl since we were freshman, sweetie. Why, is Zailey interested in round three with the Hendrix brothers?" He looks me up and down like he would enjoy a good tag team.

"Gag me, hard pass."

"I could give you something to gag on, darlin'."

"Did you get all your pick up lines from River? Or is there any part of you that holds originality, Ryder?"

"Aw, missing me already?"

I focus my gaze back on Rayce, who is slouched in a chair near the wall, not paying attention to us.

"Rayce, care to explain?"

"Fuck, Z. Come on, why do you want him when you could have me?" Ryder slugs his brother's arm as he finds a seat next to him.

"I don't want either of you. I would like a clear reason why the boy hates me." Grabbing a chair across the room.

"What? No way, no way! She doesn't know?" Ryder gets up and starts clapping his hands together.

"Cool it, man, do you ever get sick of outing me?" Rayce must be used to his brother being an attention dick.

"What don't I know? Outing you? Like...wait, are you gay?" My jaw could not have dropped closer to the ground.

All he does is shrug with open arms.

"Are you telling me that Rayce, the youngest Hendrix brother, likes men? Do not get me wrong, but damn, baby, you are the finest one out of all of them." All his brothers are good-looking sons of bitches but, Rayce is in a realm of his own.

"Yeah, crazy, right!" Ryder has an insane grin on his face. Something strikes him, and his eyes change, and he exits quickly before I can ask.

"Rayce, are we talking bi-sexual status or we talking full-on lie with thy husband kind of commitment?" I pull my chair in front of him, so our knees are touching.

"Do you think Sawyer was raped?" I back away the minute he spells her name. "Or maybe she was molested just like you were?" This time, there is full eye contact; he doesn't back down.

"Maybe it was a way for her to control the punishment she received. Did you ever think of what led her to start touching you?" I shake my head; he says it so clear, and I wonder why he is doing this.

"I—I don't want to know...it doesn't change what happened." He sulks forward, and I curl into a ball, hoping he won't continue.

"Why wouldn't you want to know? Aren't you curious about her side of the story?" His arms corrall me in, and I move my chin up to meet his eyes.

"Why does it matter?" Strangled with a stutter, frightened of the past.

"Sides of the story matter, for example. If you ask Ryder over there what happened to Sawyer when she died, he will say she drove off a cliff. If you ask River, he will punch you in the jaw." He leans to stand straight, giving me a chance to breathe.

"But, if you ask me Zailey, or you talk with our mother, we both agree that Sawyer died before your car hit bottom." Rayce grabs a chair and brings it forward next to mine.

"See, we think that before the car left the road, she had already decided. But what would make her veer off right at that very moment? What was it you said to her that made her alter your lives?"

"I—I told her that it was okay, that I was going to go away. Somewhere she couldn't get to me anymore."

"Where, Zailey, where were you going to go?"

"To heaven." I shouldn't have said it out loud. It was a prayer to be given that destination. But all the cryptic areas told me the suckers who stole their own lives would only be condemned to hell.

It breaks the dam that holds everything back. The secrets, the lies, it unfolds, and I collapse. Rayce's arms circle me, and I can't hold myself up to run away.

"Shh...shh. My dad found out I was gay, he threw me up against the wall and tried to strangle me. My mother held a shotgun to his face. Ryder, my twin over there, he hung me out to dry." His whispers cover my hair, and I feel the smooth syllables scatter through my roots.

"Why would he betray you?" My tears soak his shirt.

"Ryder caught us messing around."

"Who?"

"Lox Rutledge, his best friend."

"No way! Now I know you are an incredibly hot piece of ass, but, there is no way that Lox, all-American blue-blooded boy, is swinging your way." I remove myself and plaster on that pretend face I've been so brilliant to create.

Rayce looks at me, trying to figure out how I snapped back so quickly. Wondering if he can still trust me.

"Yeah, surprise." His thumb grazes his chin, shifting his focus on Ryder, who is trying to chat up Anika.

"Come on, you've got to share more."

"Why do I? You don't want to share your secrets. Maybe we should keep our pep talks to a minimum, babe." He smacks my leg as he walks out of the art room back to the common area.

Chapter 8

RIVER

This yard is not one I thought I would be standing on the edge of ever again. Especially not with the brutal truth I am about to face.

There is no reason.

Okay, one reason, I need to know.

Sawyer's dad flicks his head up when he hears my jeans knock against the porch railing.

"River? How have you been, son?" He stands tall and brushes off his hands, wiping the sweat of garden work out of his eyes.

"Is it true?" Not here for pleasantries, or catching up on the bull shit of old days.

We stare at each other; he doesn't respond.

"Maybe Miranda is home; should I talk to her?"

Again, the silence suffocates as we wait for an explanation. This is the worst, the tight energy around us. Sawyer's dad debates how to defend his daughter without incriminating her.

One final nod. "Follow me around back, son."

He stands in front of the deck, while I find a step on the stair.

"Is it true, what Zailey said in that letter, is it true?"

"Yes." Quick and cutthroat.

FUCKKKKK.

Ruined, the bottom of the barrel guts bloody last breath. Fuck, I'm an idiot, freaking fool.

"You've got to be kidding me. I just ruthlessly dismantled Zailey beyond recognition."

"Zailey wasn't the only victim. There were others."

"Did you hear me, Warren? I called her a liar, accused her of making it up. Sawyer molested her best friend. Shit, I think I am going to be sick." My guts twist, and I heave up breakfast.

Asshole, bastard, motherfucker, none of these names even come equal to the definition of who I am right now.

"Are you okay?"

"River? Is that you? Let me get some water." Miranda calls through the back screen door.

"Did you say she wasn't the only one?"

Another nod from Warren.

"There were a couple kids she babysat; their parents came forward after she died. I guess word got out about Zailey's suicide note."

"How bad?"

"Not near the degree of what happened to Zailey, not as long either. For them, it was a one-time thing. Zailey's letter...it must have been happening—"

"For years." God, how awful do I feel? My brain is boiling, and my skin needs to be replaced.

"We were in the wrong. She had just died; we lost our only child. We said things to Zailey we shouldn't have."

Miranda arrives with a wet towel and a glass of water. I set them down next to me, making sure any other information won't wreck me.

"Why, why would Sawyer do that? Was she...did something happens to her?"

"We assume something may have happened with a fifth grade teacher back when we lived in Kentucky. There had been other reports. But when we asked her, she said no." Miranda looked across the yard to a rusted swing set.

"There weren't any alarming signs or changes in her behavior. We believed her when she said nothing happened. Maybe there were signs we didn't pick up on; it's hard to think back. Sawyer was always an obedient girl, never gave us much fuss."

"What happened to the teacher?"

"Went to jail for eight years, out now for good behavior."

"Piece of shit."

"We're sorry, we assumed it was a lie too. We've tried reaching out to Zailey to apologize."

"She tried to kill herself over this! Over us, not believing her cries for help. You assumed? I demanded her to take back what she said. I nearly spit in her face with disgust. We forced her to believe someone else was more important, even though they were doing something wrong."

"Hey, if we could take it back, we would."

"But you can't, can you? Neither can I. None of us can ever make it right again. You lost your daughter because she was going to make sure Zailey went down in flames with her. All because Zailey had enough of being abused. She wanted to be free." I look to the sky and find no relief in the warmth of sunshine burning my eyes. "But all we did is force her to remain in prison, locked behind bars."

Two Years Later

Chapter 9

RIVER

"A mos? You want to hit the gym before practice?" I knock on his door, and I hear Aspen say no. As I turn, the door opens, and he grabs a hoodie following me out.

"Amos, it's my birthday, you bastard." Aspen, his on-and-off again, chick hollered through the wall.

"It's her birthday?"

"Whose?" Down the sidewalk, a couple blocks from the gym, he honestly looks up at me, confused.

"Aspen said that while we were leaving."

"Oh, yeah, maybe I guess." Amos' eyes are focused in front. Lost on reality, living nightmares of his past.

"Did you get her something?"

"She isn't my girlfriend." A shrug, most I've gotten out of him for a week.

"She'll expect something, women always expect these things."

"Fuck, then you get her something."

"I'm not the one sleeping with her." His shaggy hair shakes a bit like he is exhausted with the conversation.

"I don't want to be anyone to anyone. I just don't know how to get rid of Aspen. She wants something I can't give her."

"Commitment?"

"A future."

"Who has that?" When I reach for the door, he looks up at me, trying to gauge if I can use this against him.

"Harper, my Calico girl, owns all timelines, even those ones I pretend are mine."

"Whose Harper?"

"She's—"

"Hold on, man, let me grab this call. I'll meet you there."

It's her.

Zailey's name pops up on my screen. 3 years earlier, the same name appeared, calling frantic about my girlfriend lying at the bottom of the hill.

Should I answer?

Two, three, four rings. I wait. Wondering if the next voice I hear will be frantic with need or collected with reverence.

"Hello?"

"River? Um, hey, it's..."

"Zailey?"

"Hi, River. It's been a while."

"Some good years."

"Right, I was just calling because your brothers told me where you go to school. We recently moved here, and I wanted to meet up." Her voice seems sour with insecurities.

"We?" The only word I hear in her statement; besides, she's here. I look out around the streets, wondering if she is lurking from a distance.

"My friend and I, we met when we were at the same therapist." She giggles a little, and someone calls her stormy.

"I would love to meet up, that's great to hear. Rayce and Ryder transferred closer to home; it'll be nice to have someone."

"Well, we both needed a fresh start, so here I am. I hope I don't cramp your style."

"You could never."

"I'll call you soon, River. We were just taking a break from unpacking."

"Alright, see you around, Z."

For once, the Earth seems to be balanced, and I can walk in a straight line, not worried about casualties. As I enter the gym, I see Amos' head down as his hands try to break his skull.

"Okay, dude?"

But he isn't listening: in the next second, he has two guys next to us pinned against the mirrors.

Not saying anything but intimidating them all the same.

"Check your friend, man."

"I'm not in control of other's actions. If Amos wants to beat your ass, then that is considered free will." I take a sit on the weight bench and lean back.

"Don't ever fucking come near me again."

"Sure, psycho."

"Want to spot me?" Wiggling under the bar, getting into position.

My roommate takes a few more breaths and tries to gain composure as his chest heaves.

"You didn't try to stop me."

"Come on, after all these years, all the other fights I've broken up, why would this one make any difference? It's your choice to mess up and stay straight."

"Why is there a big grin on your face?"

"A girl from back home called and wants to hook up. She and her friend just moved here."

"Threesome, huh? I don't know how you have that much confidence to please multiple partners at once."

"Nah, it won't be like that. Maybe get a nice suck on my dick for old times' sake."

"High school girlfriend?"

"She was a friend of my ex."

"The charm you have on people. I never see the appeal." He starts laughing and lifts up the bar.

Before he got on the bench, he added nearly triple the weight, and now I'm the one who's laughing.

"No way you can lift that much, man."

"Speak for yourself bro, I did ten reps yesterday with more."

"Prove it."

And the asshole does, and he calls me cocky.

"Getting serious with Aspen?" My hands are deep in my front pockets, I try to cool my nerves. We are minutes away from facing a woman from my past.

One girl, I demolished with my stubborn ignorance over a futile episode. Now I hope there isn't too much damage that has been done.

"No." Stating the obvious in his mind.

"You guys said I love you."

Amos' laughter cripples him. "No, I didn't. Fuck, what a nightmare that would be to fall in love again. I learned my lesson the first fucking time, and it did not end well, Mr. Hendrix. Goddamn, I forget how fucking funny you are."

"When we were leaving, she said I love you, Amos, and you said you too." My face scrunches up in confusion.

"It doesn't mean anything. Aspen says that a lot; most of the time, I hum in agreement. River, you know me, we are going to be a bachelors for life with the relationships that messed us up."

"Scared me for a minute there, man." Aspen is an annoying presence in everybody's life.

When we get closer, I forget about their declarations. I stare forward and see her, Zailey, with her shoulders back, confident, and relaxed. A beautiful smile reaches the tops of her teeth as she sees me coming.

"River, this is my friend I was talking about. Transferred here yesterday." Her hair is different, but goddamn if she doesn't spark my chest ablaze.

"Hi, nice to meet you. What did you say your name was?" I give a hand to her friend, who is also a pretty woman.

As Amos takes in our introduction, he looks over Zailey without care. But when he hits his sight on Harper, all hell breaks loose.

"Cali?" Amos practically begs out the name.

"Shaymus." Zailey's friend looks straight at my room-mate's face.

"Your name is Shaymus! No wonder you go by Amos. That is super Celtic, dude. Wait until I tell the guys, they will not let you live this down." My eyes bounce between the two, and I laugh as his full name is thrown into the mix.

Dirty little secrets are revealed.

Zailey tries to quiet me, but I take her in my arms and hug her from behind, holding her tight. I missed her more than she wants to know. I hope my dick doesn't remind her.

As the two in front of us continue to become reacquainted, I take my time looking over the beauty in front of me. Epic waves are going on between Harper and Amos. But I am so focused on Zailey in my arms again, I can't feel the tide.

"I've missed you, Z." Bend my head down to her ear, making sure she hears me clearly.

"No, you haven't, liar."

"You're all I think about, you're home to me." Sweetness drips from my tongue, and I can't stop how charming I've become. Hopefully, it isn't coming off like I am trying too hard. Or it sounds like crap.

"River, don't tease me."

"Would never, darling. Only if it brought that wonderful smile to your face."

She must be paying attention to our friends in front of us. Zailey shouts at Amos, I defend him, and I guess I am out of the best blow job I'll ever get.

"What the fuck, man?"

"Chick was psycho, find somebody that doesn't look like a cartoon witch." Amos moves away as I watch Zailey walk away with Harper, who seems to have a limp.

I'm left standing there between two worlds, my current and past. Only it's the future I want to bring both together.

Zailey was here, she was back in my life. Forgot what her presence was like near me. It was a rush; it was getting back on the field after the final game.

~

There it was the relief of spending time with her; a huge grin shines on my face, my goddamn cheeks hurt.

A memory comes to me, and I find it relaxing, instead of pushing it away.

Zailey pretends to choke and clench her heart as she throws on the dramatics. I'm there next to her swift to catch the fall.

"When was the last time you had caffeine? Or is it chocolate this time? DEAR LORD, doesn't anybody have a chocolate bar that can save my lover's young life?" Giggling, at my comment, brings her back to life; she relaxes in my arms.

"Thank Jesus, ladies, and gentlemen, it was just gas! Just passing some heavy, smelly ass gas!" Waving us away from the crowd as she smacks my shoulder. "What would you do without me keeping you entertained all the time?"

"Probably live up to my calling and achieve a lot of success." My banter is always locked and loaded.

"Rude!"

But with a good mood like that, the other shoe drops on my junk. Causing the pain to resurface into a panic.

"She's dead." My speech is soft as I sitting on my bed. The curve of my spine arching over as I stared into the wall.

"What? Who died?" Amos' voice is confused, and I can hear him rustling to adjust. He reaches for his clock. I nod at the 4 o'clock hour, beaming bright.

His voice seemed heavy and panicked. I wonder if his nightmares were faced the same way as the ones I saw. But in my vision, two girls were dedicated to destroying my ability to hope.

No longer powerful, I let my body go limp on top of the mattress. Vibrating the floor throughout our room. Right now, I didn't want to think about Zailey. I tried to ask philosophical questions about where we go after we die. Or bring up conspiracies. I didn't want to face her.

Even through the alcohol mask, the image got more precise, and she saw all the flaws inside that I made sure no one knew I couldn't defend.

"Zailey Jensen, I loved her first, but that makes me an asshole because my girlfriend is six feet under." My confession comes out in a moonlit sigh; fuck it felt good to say it out loud.

Amos shifts on his side of the room and sits up.

"Bailey Hansen? Who's that? That girl Harper hangs out with? I thought her last name was Jensen or something." His voice goes from confused to irritation, and I wonder if he is worried about Harper, the girl that Z hangs around with ever since.

"Jensen, Zailey, with a Z. Her best friend Sawyer Patterson, she...she was my girlfriend. When I was seventeen." Every last drop of that whiskey is gone into my veins. The clank of an empty bottle makes an echo, and our room feels small.

"Seventeen? Bro, are you okay?"

"It's her birthday." Now both of us laying flat. Our minds spinning with anxious worry for different reasons.

"October twelfth. It's a good day to be born."

"Isn't it, though? I love October. I love her. I keep wondering if I will ever stop. You know? I have this death grip on her image in my head. Never wanting to let her slip through my fingers again. If I forget her..." Waterworks come out stray bullets to my pride. I don't ever want to remove the idea of who I thought Sawyer really was. I can't forgive myself for not knowing what she had done to Zailey.

But there I go, floating with my eyes closed in denial. If what Zailey said was true, then I can't get over the fact I stood by and allowed it to happen.

"How do you do it? How do you forget her?" Needing to know, I was desperate to understand how he covers up people in his life. Driving past their presence like they were only tourists on a road trip.

"You don't, I haven't. I lie to myself, mostly. You don't have to forget her." But he did it so well, with her the girl he dethrones and belittles. His parents, his family. One day I worry I'll lose my friend because he might realize he won't need me either.

"I am in this conflict because of Zailey; I think I am falling in love with her, and I don't want to. I want so badly to push her away like all of the rest. But she looks at me, she gives me this stare like she understands everything inside me. Things I can't speak about." Referring to the shame, the regret, the kind of emotions that keep you captive. Just to make you understand how much of a prisoner you are for your wrongdoings.

"Well, everybody has to move on at some point." A part of me knows I should seek advice elsewhere, but at least he isn't shutting down.

"But not you."

"Yeah, I am the anomaly." Amos' thoughts are out in the open and I believe the shadow demons I heard Harper talking to Zailey about, are what is clouding my judgments.

"She wanted to ride back with her friends. My buddies and I were in the car ahead of the girls. We were up at Black Canyon, and there is this high curve on the mountain. No guard rail, just empty air; they rolled. We stopped our car. And all of us, could do nothing but watch in humiliating horror as they rolled. Their screams, oh God, their haunting screams. Sounds you never get out of your mind.

"You know what the fucked up thing was? Sawyer was the only one that died. No seatbelt confined her. The only one thrown from the car. By the time we got down the hill, her body was cold. Frozen brilliantly. She looked beautiful so preserved. Like she would stay that way forever."

"Fuck, River. That is some messed up shit right there."

"Sometimes, I feel like I am going insane. Like I talk to Sawyer in my head or have conversations. Just to keep the feeling of her alive. All I want is her, and she's gone. How can I go on? Why do I get to be happy? Why, Amos? Why did this happen?" My eyes burn with no loyalty to my ego; they fume with the chance at freedom.

"I don't know why, man. I haven't a fucking clue why shit happens to good people. I can't even begin to tell you that it will be okay. Because I don't know that. I don't know anything, man. It's been two years, and I can hardly look at my reflection."

"Harper?" I ask, and in the dim light, I see his head go up and down. Bringing her name up, because he isn't the only one that doesn't have the balls to be brave.

"Dude, you've got to grovel. You need to get over yourself and win her over. Or at least move on to someone new. What you are doing right now, it isn't healthy for you. The hot and cold act. I'm sure it's confusing as hell to keep up with."

"My head hurts. But I know I don't want anybody new."

"Just have to convince her she doesn't need anybody new."

"Amos, you are my best friend."

"River, best bud too." We bump fists while we try and wipe away the tears.

"A bunch of freaking vaginas around here." Preacher opens the door and closes it.

Chapter 10

RIVER

When we get to the curve of the lake near my family's cabin, I start to second guess that maybe this was a horrible, terrible idea.

Zailey hasn't stopped jabbering. I thought I was doing Amos a favor. But, pretty Harper girl hasn't said two words since we decided to head out on this weekend getaway.

When we arrive, the girls get out and head inside.

"Hey, Amos. Sorry, I thought maybe you and Harper would have some time to talk on the way down. But I guess Zailey stole the limelight. She tends to do that often." I rub my forehead with the back of my knuckles, trying to figure out how to give my best friend a break.

"No worries, man. I didn't talk to her for two years. I think I can handle a couple hours of radio silence." He acts cool, but his stare lingers after her.

We grab some bags and head for the door.

"RAYCE!" Harper jumps into the arms of my brother.

Fuck, how do they know each other?

"It's okay, he's my brother." I tap the back of his shoulder, trying to calm him down.

I see Rayce's eyes gleam with an evil look as he stares at Amos. He must know of his and Harper's past.

My brother brings my best friend's girl up to his face. He kisses her like there is no tomorrow, and I mean, I'm impressed, considering.

"What the fuck?" Amos drops the bags and heads over to them.

"He's gay!" Grabbing his shoulder before my brother gets the beat down of a lifetime.

There's a playful banter back and forth between friends. I grab Zailey and haul her in the back bedroom with me.

I kick the door shut and watch as she crawls on the bed and looks around.

"Remember the last time we were here?" I stare at her with an appetite I hope never gets content.

"Yeah, you called me Sawyer." Her head snaps to me, and then her eyes roam the room.

My palms rub my face as I drag it down. "Before that happened, we were having a good time, babe."

"Were we? I can't remember that far back. Must have blocked it out." She lies on her back and stares at the ceiling.

Shouting begins to happen down the hallway, and before I can explain anything to Zailey, I race out the door.

When I make it to the living room, I see Harper smack a good one to Ryder's face.

"Harp?" She hasn't ever snapped in front of me.

Apologies come out of her mouth as we watch her crumble. Amos is down next to her comforting her at a distance.

"What the fuck happened, Ryder?" We are chest to chest, Rayce watches with a toothpick in his mouth. Guess the twins aren't as close as they used to be.

"It was a misunderstanding. We were weak back then, used people. Not that you were used, Harper. Fuck, it was just something to fill the void. Like Zailey and me having fun."

Zailey and him? My brother Ryder and my girl?

"Come again, little man?"

"Oh shit! She didn't tell you? Listen, River, please, it was a long time ago, years even. We were all messed up; you know how she was. I would have never done that to you."

This time, I harness the Hendrix temper, not something I am used to, but there it is. Coming full circle as I shove him outside.

"Seems the only thing you are good at these days is betraying your brothers." I pull off my shirt and take a step forward.

"River, what the hell are you doing? Why is Harper on the ground?" Zailey yells from the screen door.

I don't look back to her, because if I do, all I will see is Sawyer. And I can't make that same mistake. Wondering and waiting why the fuck I am so damn stubborn to see the truth.

"You fucked him," I yell back at her. She doesn't say a word and has the decency to sigh.

Rayce is on my side gives me a nod saying it's okay to beat the shit out of his mirror image. I guess this was a long time coming.

"Who's going to save you now, baby boy? Ain't seen Daddy in a couple months. Maybe Mommy will forgive you after you get spanked a few times."

"We aren't really going to have a showdown right now, are we?" His words sound annoyed, but I know the asshole is scared.

He must think we are kidding, and I laugh a little bit before I gut punch him and shove him to the ground.

"Did we forget to give you the message? Being loyal to blood is a given, but not fucking around with our brothers' lives, that last one seems like it's going to be a doozy for you to grasp, Ryder." I bend down to his ear, making sure he feels equally disgusted.

"I'm sorry." The comeback spits out.

"Be down at the lake." Not caring who's listening.

The dirt road is littered with stones, and I pick up one after the other. When I reach the shore, I throw them as hard as I can. Remembering what a baseball back in the little league felt like in my hands.

Every rock I fling skims the surface and creates the ripple effect. Sawyer's death, another ripple. Sex with Zailey, another. Making Zailey smaller than the scum of the earth, triple whammy.

"River," Harper calls as she rounds the tree by the shore.

"Did you know?" Not looking at her as I try to erase all the odd ripples and even out the water to make our problems go away.

"No." When I check over my shoulder, she makes herself comfortable on a log.

"Seems fate has other plans than giving us a chance to be something." It isn't fate. First, it was Sawyer, then it was me, and now the torch passed back to Zailey. Who seems to be using it to burn down our worlds?

"No, it seems Zailey keeps running interference with what is inevitably come to present." Her friendship with Zailey seems to be braided with imperfection. Both marred with past scars, the pain still present.

"She doesn't want me, never has." Even I know it sounds like a fib.

"Nobody knows what she wants, not even her."

"I am out of chances, resources, clues. Damnit, Harper, we aren't made for each other. The more I sit here and wait, Ryder and her have the same destructive personalities. The seductive control makes them feel powerful; they're the same." My final battle cries.

"Me too."

I give up with the metaphors and rocks and find a seat next to her.

"Why do you keep trying then?"

"No more about her, please." I flinch thinking about Ryder on top or behind Zailey.

All she does is nod.

"Why does Shaymus?"

"He can't help it." It seems we are both in a trembling phase of trying to recover what was best for us.

"One day, it has to stop; eventually, the pulse will weaken, our memories will fade, giving place to new ones." Harper closes her eyes and focuses on something else.

"What's so funny?" Harper laughs, and it lightens my mood a great deal.

"She is laughing at my laugh." Amos comes out of the woods. The grin on his face makes my anger dwindle a little more.

"Your laugh?" Confused as hell, these two have some type of telepathy.

"Yeah, the first time Harp came down the hallway, I was busting a gut in a fit of laughter. Tears blinding, I was laughing so hard. When I caught my breath and looked up, she was standing there smiling." Amos goes on with his story as he takes a spot next to me.

"How adorable." Here I am, the 3rd wheel.

"Don't be an ass, tell us when the first time was you saw Z?" Amos shoves my shoulder while I knock into Harper. "Sorry, Harp."

"I was making out with her best friend, Sawyer. Out of the corner of my eye, I see this chick death glaring me. So, I stop sucking face to look at the mood killer. First, she looks at Sawyer and then back to me. She looks fierce, but then a smile grows on her face. If I had known what that smile meant, I probably would have never touched her friend again."

"Death threat smile?" Harper questions like she already knows the look that powers Zailey.

"Level the playing field, even the odds, balance the score." My friends nod along with me, understanding what it really means to have the wild girl with colored hair in our lives.

"It made me horny as hell; you know me, Amos, I am already amped up on the regular, but throw in a defiant catalyst, and I near damn shot my load in my shorts while I had my future girlfriend sitting on my lap." Remembering Zailey for the first time makes me crave her.

"Dude, don't bring me into your obsession with sex." Amos tries to bridge a gap between our sexual adventures as college men.

"What? Don't act alarmed by it; you of all people should understand. Damn, our first year, we hit records I could never dream." My glory days make my spirits spike.

"Man..." My best friend hits my chest, and I just swallow my laugh.

"Right, sorry. Excuse me, I am going to find Zailey." Smacking my jeans as I take off all the debris.

"Glad you decided to talk things out." Amos tries to be encouraging, his smallest effort.

"There won't be any talking. Bad things happen when that chick speaks her mind. Her mouth says a lot of bitchy shit she doesn't mean. Am I upset that fucker of a little brother tapped an ass that belongs to me? Sure as hell I am, but make up sex is the best, and I promise she will be sorry for a long time." A hint of excitement hits my head as I think about all the forgiveness Zailey will be begging me for by the end of the night.

Chapter 11

ZAILEY

"Harper, I swear I meant to tell you. It didn't mean anything. I came back from my mom's house, and he was standing outside smoking. I was weak, Harp, he taunted me." They always mock me, in ways I have to prove them wrong or prove them right.

The night I came home, exhausted from fretting over my mother and brother's well-being. It wasn't the first time I let Ryder sneak under my suspicions before.

Ryder was puffing out some good smelling weed; the smell lured me in with the same smile the smoker did.

"Your girl gave me quite the ride earlier." I knew it was wrong, but it was tempting. I took the blunt from his lips, and I sucked in hard until it torched my lungs. "So, you want to get out of here?"

"You literally just had your dick in my best friend's vagina."

"I remember a girl back in high school who loved to have a good time." He glanced over to me, the challenge in his eyes.

Hate, it covered my insides and pumped through my blood. What was one more discretion? It wasn't like Harper and Ryder were going to run into the sunset together? Besides, we'd been down this road before.

"Sure, get me something stronger, though."

I never was afraid, until I saw it swirling in the eyes of my mother, as she lay dying. There wasn't a chance I missed that look, the fearless being before me was crumbling, and her only approach was defeat.

An assignment they made us do at therapy, share something we learned from our guardians. I choose to fear because I saw the most courageous woman be cut down, and in her eyes, I saw the strain of never getting back up again.

It hurt more than a lover stomping on my heart with definite venom, betraying the only friend who was there for me.

I pace back and forth in the room where River took my virginity. Of course, it was here. Here is where Ryder decided to out his brother, making his father remove Rayce from the family.

And here where Ryder had to spill the beans to Harper and River. Every time I try to stand on my feet, I keep getting knocked back down.

"Maybe this is a good thing, everything is out in the open, and we can all move on." The reasons I convince myself are reasonable and won't bury me.

"Move on from what?" River comes in the door, not a bit surprised that I am still here.

"From what happened." The bed dips where I find a place.

Chapter 12

RIVER

"A lot of new information coming into light." I slip off my jeans and crawl into the bed next to where she sits.

"Does it change how you feel?"

"Nothing has before, so why would it now?" Peeking at me under her eyelashes. I tap the bed next to me, and she moves to the other side.

"It's okay to tell me what you want sometimes."

"Why?" I'm suspicious, but I shouldn't be. It's the first reaction I have.

"Because sometimes, I can give you those things."

"Why are you so loyal?" Her head rests on my chest, my fingers tangle in her hair.

"Born and bred that way. Except Ryder forgot who he came from."

"It was twice." I snuggle closer to him, hoping it gives him comfort. I don't know how to be the comforter.

"It doesn't matter if it was a million times." I give her a kiss on the head.

"Did your dad really try to choke Rayce when he found out he was gay?" Her voice almost squeaks, and I stiffen, not wanting to roam over the minefield.

"My dad isn't a bad guy. He grew up in a different time. Things have changed, and he has a hard time accepting them. The same thing happened when a few of my brothers brought home women from different backgrounds."

Blinking away the images as the insults from my father are flung at my brothers' spouses.

"Your dad is a bigot! He told your brother he wished he was dead rather than like men!" She doesn't move, but accuses and screams all the same.

"What do you want me to say?"

"Stop defending him if he is in the wrong."

"Would you stop defending your mom? Do you ever defend Sawyer's parents?"

"We can't talk about this anymore." We couldn't, especially since I hadn't confessed our final sin. One last nail in the coffin that floats us from our past.

"There is going to be a day when you wake up and decide that picking yourself also means picking me, Zailey.

Choosing to love yourself in all the ways I do means freely giving up the assumption that I was born to break you and make you mine."

Sweet sighs exit her lips. I continue to whisper as she dozes.

"It means trusting, Zailey. Hoping two worlds you wish you could scorch and carve murderous words into won't become reality. But that means that you finally realize every time you've been guarding your heart, so have I. Every minute you left early to protect against something unknown, I also was doing the same." When I look down at her face, I memorize every line, hoping this will make us immortal.

"For one day, I want you to realize that I've been choosing myself in efforts and with the end goal of always choosing you to be a part of me." Bending my head down to meet her lips so soft, to seal the promise.

When I pull away, I nuzzle in closer, and I wait for this dream together to become a reality.

"Zailey, your feet are tickling me." I casually bump her with my butt for her to adjust herself. "Z, you've got to move those cold ass toes off my back, babe." My fingers poke her sides.

Whatever I did was the wrong thing to do; her eyes open wide. Shock and horror cover her features, and I am drenched in terror.

"Where am I? How my gosh, how did I get here?" Scrambling to the corner, her chest heaving. "No, no, not here. Why did you bring me back here? I can't be here, did you do this to me?"

"Z, calm down; everything is okay." Whipping the sheet off as I make my way around the bed to come near her.

"Is she here? Is Sawyer behind that door? She told me one last time, and I did it. I said no more. Are you in this with her? Did you drug me?" A high-pitched screech follows her hysteria.

"What the hell, babe, seriously?" I am a few feet from her, an attempt to reach out.

"Don't touch me, stay away from me! Help! Help! Help, somebody, help me!" Her palms try to slap my efforts away.

"Zailey, stop yelling. It's the middle of the night. Come back to bed, you need to relax. You are going to hyperventilate." Keeping the distance between us a safe amount.

"Did you touch me? Stay away from me. Please don't do it again. She promised it was over." Zailey looks chaotically over her body, seeing if any marks are visible.

"Zailey? Are you okay?" A knock and a head pop through, showing us Rayce.

"Man, I think she's having an episode." Shoulders slump down as I put my hands in the pockets of my sweatpants.

Down on the wooden floor, I watch the frayed edges of the rug as I attempt to pinpoint the time when I became the enemy.

"RAYCE! Oh no, do they have you in on this too?" Tears begin to bubble and boil over, fear hiking the energy of the room.

"No, Z. Nobody is going to hurt you. Remember, I like guys." Rayce is calm, not tempted by her panic.

"You're gay? No, how did they get you? It's always the most beautiful one. You are the hottest Hendrix brother. I slept with Ryder because he looks a little like you and River."

"Zailey, I need you to breathe." Not going near her, just asking. When her breath doesn't simmer, he looks to me. "River, you need to go get Harper."

"No, I should stay." What use is leaving if I can't be a hero or helping hand in her downfall?

"He came here with her; they're planning something together."

"No, Sawyer's gone, remember? She drove off the road." I watch as my brother stands next to her, explaining reality.

"I was supposed to die in the car. She was trying to kill me." Zailey bites on the tips of her nails.

"Come here, baby girl, everything is okay." He beckons her, but she isn't convinced.

"Rayce, you can't let her get to me. I'm going to be free. They can't get to me if you stay with me, promise me; you'll be here." She clings closer to where he stands.

"Zailey, what's wrong?" Harper's long hair follows as she greets the unstable girl cowering next to the wall.

"Who is she? No, you promised me I would be safe." Light brown eyes flutter over her best friend before refusing her presence.

"Zailey, you are safe." Harper isn't worried about the strange behavior.

Am I the only one freaking the fuck out?

"Rayce, River is on her side. She told me so many times. She said he knew what we did together, what she did, and didn't care. He can't be here." The finger she points at me might as well be a straight shot to the heart.

"Zailey, do you want any candy? How about apple bottom butts, strawberry cheeks, sweet muffin tops, and Jell-O drool."

A colossal concoction of nonsense words filters out of Harper's mouth as she tries to connect with my girl.

"Harper..." With a few blinks, her breath quiets down, and her eyes refocus on everybody in the room.

"Come back to me." It was a small whisper, the most remarkable plea, I could beg.

"I never leave." Those places that haunt her most. She thinks I was an accomplice to the tragedy.

"I got it from here, boys. She'll be okay. Isn't that right, Zailey?" Harper has her calmed down, an arm around her shoulder as she makes a way to the mattress.

"Turn the tables over for sunflower shamrocks; you'll find the dish of sugar is the doctors treat." Zailey continues on with a symbolic song only those two can decode.

"What the fuck is that?" Nerves are getting the best of my patience, the whole scene making me anxious.

No one seems to be picking up how upset I am right now.

"She's fine. It's a song we made up to calm down. Our psych was called Dr. Candy. Z, where are your pills?"

"I don't need one." Those beautiful lips pout.

"It'll help you feel better, at least for tonight." Soothing her hair back as she points to her bag on the ground.

"Okay. You'll stay with me?" Zailey still not looking in my direction. Harper nods and climbs on the bed as Zailey lays her head down on her lap. "I'm sorry I'm a freak."

"Yes, rude awaken siren." Rayce's twin hollering down the hallway.

"Fuck you, Ryder," Zailey huffs through a strangled throat.

"It seems like she is doing fine. I am headed back to bed. I've got a flight in the morning back to the university."

Rayce brushes a hand over her cheek and gives her a soft temple kiss.

"Thanks, Rayce, for everything."

"You, Zailey Jensen, are worth sacrificing sleep." He exits the room, and I don't know what I should do, so I leave too.

Without asking if she is okay or needs water. All I hear as I shut the door is her quiet farewell.

"Goodnight."

Chapter 13

ZAILEY

"Did you get enough sleep?" My mind has been awake for hours. I followed every swirl on my ceiling's texture.

We were back in our apartment, and there wasn't much I could get out of my head. Except for the round of freak out mode in the middle of the night.

My ass was planted on the kitchen counter. Harper stopped when she saw me. She even yawned before a sigh was let go, and she faced me.

"I got a sufficient amount. Maybe you need to focus on your own moon cycles for your sleeping patterns to be optimal."

"Sorry, her mother's words come out of her mouth when she is cranky." Shaymus gives his two cents as he makes his way to the bathroom.

"Shaymus, so not nice to see you again this morning." Holler my statement before the door closes.

"Soon you won't have to, I hear you, and I are going to be switching roommates." His comeback vibrates through the door.

"You're moving out?" My face stays neutral, the shock hitting my body in various parts of my back.

"It's time." Right into my eyes, like she means it.

But she can't honestly move out. She wouldn't, would she?

"Not with him? It's only been a few months; you can't trust him that quickly. We've stuck by each other's side; we can't just stop now. Harp, come on this is ridiculous." Panic sets in, and I rush to make it all routine.

"Zailey, I have stood by your side through everything. I was there every time you pushed River, Olallie, and me away. When is it going to stop? I need to breathe, even if it doesn't work out with Shay. We need this...this space."

"Oh, it's going to work out." Shaymus making his statements. Harper doesn't even turn around to correct him.

"When will you stop being mad at me? I said I was sorry for what I did with Ryder. It was selfish." I chuck my bowl of cereal in the sink, fed up with this tension between us.

"It isn't about Ryder." Harper's mouth gives me a soft, cautious smile.

"Then what is it about? Tell me so I can fix our friendship." We are all each other have left.

"You, Z, it's about you. I've barely been keeping my head above water the last couple of months and the stress of having to hold you up along the way, well, it's exhausting. And I know you think that's awful, but it's TRUE. We can't be each other's crutches." She grabs clothes off the floor and starts putting them in a backpack.

"Olallie will be upset that you've broken the balance of our triangle."

This makes her stop; she stares across the room at a picture of the three of us. Using Olallie against her is a low blow. I guess I've met darker depths.

"Olallie will understand that it was obtuse from the beginning."

I nod, staring at the floor, fully acknowledging what I've become. "You'll come back, won't you?"

"Zailey, what happened to you was extravagant. It's horrible, but we both know I can't heal you, and you can't heal me. The responsibility is solely our own."

"I'm fine." Forever the most significant falsification.

"No, you're not. It's a lie we tell ourselves hoping one day we'll wake up and it's true. Listen, that night I went to Shaymus' house with his family. My parents saw me; they, well anyway, I thought I had hit rock bottom before with what happened in the hospital, at the center. But it was a new rock bottom; the rocks didn't cut at my throat, it wasn't cold or dark. It was solitary confinement, a prison I sulked in; I realized I'm not getting out unless I learn how to climb. There is no evil force holding us down. It's just us, we are both the predators and victims." Her speech is sour. I can see the raw goodness through the cracks. She was always the right kind.

"Maybe its ADHD, they said PTSD, or maybe it's just a lack of vitamin D. Or not getting enough of the good big long D, I don't know." Avoiding the surreal talk makes me breathe a little easier.

"Make jokes all you want; we'll see you around, Z." Shaymus waits a minute before following her back to her room.

Our apartment is small; its walls are cleaned with gloss white paint. I go to my room, across the hallway from hers. Crawl into the corner, rock back and forth.

"Everything is alright. Everything is working out." My mantra comes out quiet and quick.

I hear River's truck pull up and inch my back further into hiding. So desperate for relief until the floods allow me to cry.

A mirror hangs at my side, flex and stretch my fingers as I reach the tips of my toes. I take a deep breath, count down from 10. One swoop to the left, and it's a quick nod before I move on a pass to the closet.

It's a thing with reflections. They make me nervous; too many ghosts stand behind me, and I can't remember the curses to send them away.

Sometimes, I see past my own eyes, deep into the depths where I no longer am free.

Blinking hard with a shake of my head, I focus on a simple outfit. Try to calm my hair from the usual spike that gets confused glares.

Vibrations start to spin my phone on the counter. Olallie's face patiently waits for me to answer; her fingernails adjusts curls to frame her look better.

I click it on. When I don't say anything, she flutters her long eyelashes and flicks a finger with the letter Z.

"I don't know what you want me to say, O. Harper won't take my calls. I've apologized a thousand times. What would you like for the conclusion to become, my silent angel?" She'll hate me because I don't give her a chance to respond as I close my eyes.

Seconds, I punish her disability with my own cruel control.

A loud noise echoes and then a shutter of a curse word.

When I look back at the screen, her eyes never waver. There aren't tears moving to be sucked up for another occasion. She peaks one manicured eyebrow and her pursed lips remind me that she is far more mature than I could ever be.

So, I forget myself, and that's when I let my fingers fling and let it all be revealed.

Some days, I feel unwell, like I see an avalanche barreling towards me, and I feel relief knowing I can't outrun it.

Hoping, pleading with it to bury me faster. I'm fucked up, and I worry I can't be fixed from the guidance of the elders. They want me to forget her. They need me to eliminate her from my memory. Like she didn't carve her name in all the fears I had as a young girl trying to believe I could survive.

My mother would be ashamed; my father too eager to interact with me less.

"Somedays, we have a choice to hold our breath until living makes sense. Or we can force the wind to penetrate our lungs, giving us another chance." This time, her words are more transparent than any reply she's given me.

Chapter 14

RIVER

We sleep on the same bed, but in between us, our backs turned on each other, holding up the Great Wall of China.

She doesn't reach over, and I stopped trying to comfort her physically. The mental strain on both of us is evident enough so that when we take ourselves outside, there are no public touches.

That's when I start peeking around, keeping a catalog of options open. Never a shortage of onlookers, most of them my taste. Mainly there is lust in their eyes as I give them a hidden side smirk.

Expressions flutter with a flirt, biting down on their bottom lip for exaggeration. They remind me how easy it' was to be loved at the moment.

But with the tug of my hand, the shame of wanting to be free shakes away the opportunity.

"River? River, I don't want to go to counseling anymore." It's not the first time she has wanted to stop therapy. I look up to the sky and try not to roll my eyes.

"Z, we talked about this and agreed it's been helping you. There has been an improvement; a few more sessions, and then you can decide. Okay?" My shoes shuffle along the concrete, walking down the block.

"Why does it even matter? No one is going to stick around anyway..."

"What'd you say?" A last glance over my shoulder to keep the image of the willing beauty from fading.

Zailey stops moving, and I go forward a bit until I halt. She peers up at my face, then over to where I was hoping to keep a memory.

"Nothing." She releases her strength, and I let her walk away.

~

"You are not kind; you are not patient. Love with you is stubborn. It's chaotic, and there is so much misery in the passion between us. Gut-wrenching punches hit my stomach every time I think of ecstasy. Like shooting my load and then having my balls in a guillotine. Wondering when you'll do me the favor of stripping the last part of dignity. You can't stand still, and I am all calm. The silence I am comfortable with makes you scream."

She lays naked, her breath intake picks up, a body full of exhales. But still, I need her closer, want to go deeper within the psychosomatic of her thinking.

"Our love is different because it wasn't our, to begin with. You don't think you deserve love, because it was hers to have and you scavenged for the crumbs. Love with me will always be, while with you it's now or never." My palm presses down on the low of her back. She arches her ass back into my groin, losing focus on the declaration.

I lean forward, smooth the hair away from the side of her face. I wrap my fingers around it and pull. Her neck wet with sweat as I bend down to lick up the grief I've been giving to her.

Lips snap at her throat, pushing my bare body against hers. Another hand finds the gap between her legs, and my fingers find the wishing well.

"What do you say, Zailey? Do you love me? Are you even capable of that emotion?" My taunt caters to the control, giving her goosebumps.

My thumb finds her ass and rubs it, kissing her bare shoulders as she stares at the mirror across the room at us.

It's then there is a smile, the slow grin that only keeps growing as she watches me discover my playground.

I slide two fingers in, and she squeezes.

"Still so tight for me, need a warm-up before I make my way back into that tunnel." The craze takes over, and

I let out a hungry growl. I'm spreading her legs, licking between moist lips, ones I know that cry for me.

Blind, it overtakes me, and I can't wait any longer until I am deep inside of her. Lifting one leg on top of my shoulder, giving her a small kiss on the ankle. The only warning as I thrust balls deep into her heaven of a home.

"Fuck, I love you, Zailey."

Another pull and push.

"You're mine, aren't you? Goddamn, I can never get enough. I love you so much."

Moans rush out of her mouth, her head falling back in orgasm, and the pulsing on my cock nearly makes me black out.

"Oh, fuck, Zailey. Baby, damn, fuck, I love you." My hands trail her curves; on her spine, a long tattoo of a curved river is carved into her skin.

Her body goes stone, knowing what I'm thinking. I gulp down another breath, hoping to erase the drowning.

"It's okay, Z, it's perfect, baby. Just for me, isn't it?" A slow slide out, and I am back making impressions in the attempt to gain freedom.

Chapter 15

ZAILEY

"Zailey, I need to tell you something." His voice is still brutally raspy from the height of sex.

"Okay, why are you so serious?" I don't turn over to face him. Instead, I close my eyes and remember how eliciting our encounter was moments ago.

"Just need to clear the air on a few things, darlin'." He kisses my head, holding my hand.

"What is it?"

"I went and saw Sawyer's parents after you got sent to that center in Fort Collins with my brothers. We had a conversation."

"Talked about what?" Hesitation grows, and I feel my insides recoil.

"I'm sorry, I should have believed you." His head hangs, and I swear I smell the disappointment seeping from his shoulders.

"Believed me?" I give him a small laugh. "Wh—What do you mean?"

"They told me about the letter you wrote to them. I...I didn't read it before, Zailey. Listen, Warren and Miranda, they said other parents came forward. You weren't the only victim; just the most severe case." His green eyes flick over at me, worried.

"What, were you saying you should have believed me?" This was a conversation I didn't want to have. Some truths didn't need revealing.

"Before, I called you names. Thought you were lying, that it was some sort of ploy. I didn't know how to accept who Sawyer was, or what she did to you." This is when I realize what conversation we are having.

I'm backed into a corner, reliving the facts that were present and on display. Information everyone wanted to cover up.

"I'm so sorry. I didn't mean to hurt you. Fuck, the last thing I ever wanted to do was hurt you. I couldn't bear it. I'm sorry, it kills me knowing the truth." River stands tall, and I can sense how misery has affected him.

My gaze finds the floor, but there isn't comfort beneath me.

"No, no, you don't get to tell me you're sorry." I full-on sob, and the hurt of heartbreak doesn't end with my tears. Soon, the awful noise ripples through my nose like I've been gutted, because maybe it's finally time to bleed.

"Tell me it wasn't just butterflies and bullshit. I didn't want romantic stars aligning kismet. I fucking need you to breathe. Without oxygen into my lungs, I could care less." River's words rush over me, begging to be believed.

But I don't have comfort for his lack of trust.

"Maybe you are right, and I'll always be wrong. But it's an argument you will have the rest of your life, while I've already moved on." Tears stop rolling, and I've given in to our demise.

Finally, the relief has been settled, and we are exhausted from trying to be something other than pure.

His speech ends, I feel as though I should too.

We both bend in pain, our hearts not strong enough to gather. Our minds are unwilling to negotiate.

So that's when I start to speak, and he begins to listen.

"I can't live in the now if tomorrow is a deadline I've already missed. All because you forgot to sign my name on the list."

Too much pressure to evolve into spontaneous when it feels like combustion.

"She does it every day, and yet you remind me of not being enough for you. It sickens me, and I've stripped every ugly lie I've told myself to keep you close, to keep you protected. But you act out, you hurt intentionally, and I beat all scars as reminders of broken faith. The biggest one; my heart. The smallest one believing we were both parts of the same team." Doctor Candy would be proud of the use of original words. The description down to the details.

"Zailey, do you know what day is tattooed on my arm?" A slow rise of his arm goes up to eye level, yet I remain unfocused.

"River..."

"Z, look at the date." Instead, I look in his eyes.

"Sawyer's virginity?" I find a shirt and pull it over my head, making my way to the kitchen. Hoping he won't follow with the maximum cruelty.

He continues on like I haven't interjected my two cents.

"September twelfth, your mom was in recovery for the second time. It was the first time you told me you loved me. It was the second time I told you I loved you."

"I never said that to you." In an instant, the day becomes apparent, and the memory invades me.

Oh my gosh, I did tell this poor sap I loved him.

"I'm so sorry I made the worst possible mistake. I've made countless. I can't help it. I keep pushing away the evidence, the truth. I had to do it; it became unbearable even thinking what happened could be a possibility." There's a grovel in there for me to understand, although I can't find a damn to give a fuck.

"Bullshit."

"Excuse me?" Excuses aren't working for me anymore, bucko.

"Everything is bullshit, being here with you after years of back and forth. It's all pointless. Wow, how long did it take you to get some guts?" I pretend to look at my wrist for the time. "Huh, it's a record, nearly four years."

"Don't say that." His low throttle of a voice quivers for the first time.

"It's the only thing left to say."

"So me being in love with you is shit, all your words are shit? Our relationship is just fucked from the beginning."

"You're damn right it is. This time, I don't care to fix it. This time I choose destruction. I require being free from you. This time River, I choose me, because you have never done that before. And I honestly hope I go down with the ship, sink to the very bottom where your pity-filled apology does not reach me."

"No, no, damnit Zailey, please give me a fighting chance. We can't give up this far."

It's when I take a step back, take a good look at the boy I first crushed on. Thinking he was the one that would take away my troubles, not contort my fears to his own.

"I—I need to go to bed." Turn down the hallway, finding our bedroom. I reach out to touch his pillow. The vacant dip reminds me of his real presence in my life. A mere impression easily can be turned over and become invisible.

The last few weeks have staggered on, we coexist. Revolving beside each other like Neptune and Pluto. One knows it's part of a bigger system, while the other knows it is destined to be forgotten.

"You need to leave." River's shirt is discarded on the floor. His hands grip a game controller, his biceps flex with new actions. The video game in front of him blaring, cuss words flying.

"What did you say, Z?"

"You need—"

"Hold on, one second, almost finished here." His green spring eyes glued to the TV screen.

Fifteen minutes pass; I wait, I feel as though I could forever.

Finally, his lives run out, and he tosses the controller on the table. Giving me his attention, for now.

"What's going on?" One arm goes to stretch around the back of the couch, leaning toward me.

The invisible magnetic pull between us still lit like a livewire.

"I think it's time you left, River." My fingers pick at the lint on my shoulder until I finish my sentence, then we meet eyes.

"Are you serious?"

"Yes."

"Wait—why?"

"I know you aren't happy here. There is no guarantee that I will be normal in any degree, at least not in the present tense. Aching for an escape, one-way ticket out of here, and now you can. We tried, River. Now it's time to move on." I can see him fighting, but remain to hold my head high.

River tries to mull over what is occurring. "But…" And that's it, that's his only quip back to fight this decision.

"Thanks for staying with me as long as you did; you have one of the greatest souls I've had the blessing to come into contact with." Why the hell do I sound so proper? On the outside, I am cold. But right now, I am a full nervous stomach of damaged goods sick.

"I will always love you, Zailey." Our hands intertwine the last time, him needing to believe it.

"How are you doing?" Harper's voice rings through the phone as I grab some pasta from the cupboard.

For the first time, I'm not annoyed by her question. I take it from a caring perspective.

It's been two months since River left. The first few weeks were a brutal battle, talking myself out of begging him to come home.

"I've been doing a lot better, been going to group every other week. Still on the meds; the new ones seem to be improving my moods. Adding exercise and other activities to help keep my mind focused." The pot on the stove begins to boil as I open the box.

"That's great, Zailey. I'm so proud of you. I know how hard it can be to be positive." If anyone does, it would be her.

"Thank you, I appreciate the support. How are things going with Shaymus?" Steam rises, and I blow on the cloud to cool it down.

"He's good, a little overprotective at times. Now that I say it out loud, he can be overbearing. Sometimes smothering, ...which is why I wanted to know if you wanted to go visit our sweet Olallie soon? I could use a break." Harper lets out a sigh, loosening her grip on the phone.

"Yeah, that sounds good. In fact, it might be just what we need."

"Good, let me know your schedule, and we can plan it out. I can get time off since I've been at the museum job for ninety days." I hear a ruffle of papers on the other end as I strain the noodles in the sink.

"Okay, I got a new job, so maybe we should go before I start training?"

"What will you be doing?"

"Um, it's a new thing in the area. I'll be a peer support specialist. Basically, a companion to those who are dealing with issues like us." My fingertips trace the lines on the countertops. Wondering if I can help anyone if I have a hard time uplifting myself.

"Zailey, that's incredible. I bet you'll be amazing, sounds perfect." My best friend's voice lifts my spirits and releases my nerves.

"You really think so? I've been terrified. I might ruin these people, or say something wrong and get fired."

"Z, there isn't another individual that I could think of that would be better."

"Thank you, Harp. I am sorry we had our rift a while back. Listen, about Ryder, there is no excuse for my behavior." It's true, my temper has been tamed, and it feels like I can breathe a little easier without the struggle to prove.

"It wasn't about him, and you know it. Don't fret, he wasn't my forever anyway."

"So do you want to drag this trip out? Drive the ten or so hours across Kansas to good ol' Oklahoma?" A few more scoops make it into my bowl. I look around, and for the first time, I get a sense of peace, not worried about being alone.

Long time coming that's for sure.

"Absolutely, my favorite past-time is spending hours looking at fields. But, yeah, I think I can manage a few days in your stinky car. My hip will suffer, but it'll be worth it."

"We could fly." The idea isn't as adventurous.

"No, let's drive. Give me more space to breathe and unwind. Besides, one of River's brothers got married, and they are throwing a bachelor party in Vegas. I guess Shay's brother is going too."

This is one reason why I love Harper. She doesn't shy away from saying his name to me. She has always believed in staring blindly into the things that have hurt us the most.

Harper's voice continues on with the details of the guys' trip. But I stop listening after his name. I wonder how he is doing. I don't ask because I know better than to punish myself.

One deep breath after the next, and I find my abdomen at ease.

"Z? Are you still there? Are you listening?"

"Sorry, spaced out."

"Where did you go? It's easier than dealing with reality most of the time. Daydreaming makes me feel wonderful."

A laugh escapes through my lips. "What were you saying?"

"Checked with work. I can get two weeks. Does that work for you?"

"Um, let me see. Yes, it should be good. My first day isn't until the fifth of next month."

"Great! I can't wait for our vacation!"

When I pull up to the house Amos and River are renting, I can see the relief in Harper's eyes as Amos holds tight to her.

This continues to last for another ten minutes.

"Goodness, you've said goodbye, want to wipe her ass while you're at it?" My own rear end is making a permanent spot on the passenger door.

I meet eyes with my best friend as she muffles a laugh, while Amos turns to glare at me.

"Stormy, I'm making sure my girl has everything to survive the apocalypse. Especially if this road trip goes badly, because it will if you're driving." There's that light pulse in his jaw that I'm sure made all the vapid girls at college frolic to him.

Snooze.

"Whoa, harsh. Didn't you know the judge gave me back my license after the second DUI?" I give him a wink and let the stormy nickname pass. Even though my hair hasn't been those screaming shades for months.

"My point exactly."

"I'm joking, it's not like I'll turn her into a lesbian and we will run away together. But, Harper has some wicked scars, and I'm into the wounded spirit."

His cocky grin loses its humor.

"Not funny."

In response, he receives the biggest eye-roll of the day.

"Oh, hey guys, Zailey. Didn't hear you pull up." River strolls up with his hands in his pocket, acting way too cold.

This makes one eyebrow perk.

"What the fuck, dude? Stop trying to play it off. You've been waiting by the window since this morning; desperate much?" Amos rubs his hands over Harper's shoulders, so intimate I turn away.

"Kind of a dick move, my friend. Thanks for throwing me under the bus."

"Never pretended to be anything different." His mouth shouts to River, who seems to be getting closer to me. "Except to you, babe." Their lips meet and continue to remain locked.

"Gag, shaking head, eye roll."

"No need to tell us your reactions, Stormy, we have eyes."

"Thumbs up, Amos. I just didn't know if you saw it while your eyes were trying to burn Harper's clothes off with that stare. A stare that looks deprived, but I know my girl has been giving you that wet twat like it will never dry up." My bestie laughs at her boyfriend's red cheeks, blushing with a twitch.

River just grunts. "So...how's everything been going?" He leans over the car hood; my eyes roam over his face.

"Good, they've been better. I finally got an interview for that job. I was on the waiting list. They offered me a position. I actually start training when we get back." It feels good to tell him about the festive events in my current settings.

"Really? That's awesome, Z." Standing to full height at this news, like he wants to provide a hug.

I fold my arms over my chest instead.

"What about you?"

A long arm reaches behind his neck to itch. "My dad got me an internship at this non-profit in Arizona. They work with mediators for the tribes on the reservation."

"Didn't know you were so altruistic?"

"Give me a break, I can be a good guy when I want to be."

"So you're leaving then?" A soft wind smooths the hair out of my face. I turn into it, lifting it toward the open sky.

"Yeah, leave tomorrow." Sensing his eyes on me, I keep mine closed.

"Well, safe travels. It sounds like it will be a beneficial experience."

"Yeah, me too. But, I mean, I'll be back in two months." He rushes out, worried that I would lose him forever.

Wouldn't dream of it, buddy.

"Okay. Right, well, Harper, get your tight tits in the car. I can't handle this awkward shit; it makes my skin crawl." Make my steps deliberate to take the long way around the car to get in the driver's seat.

"See you around."

"Call us if you need anything." Amos points his look at Harper.

"Yes, anything at all. If he doesn't answer, I will have my phone on for emergencies." River's throat struggles to swallow.

Amos shakes his head. "Dial it down there, man."

"Bye, River. I really do wish you the very best in Arizona. I hope it's what you are needing." He nods, and both guys wave as I pull out. River takes Amos in a headlock. Each wrestling as they laugh back into their house.

"Boys, they'll always be fools." Harper smirks over at me as we head out on the open road.

Chapter 16

RIVER

"I don't know if I even want to go anymore, Dad." My elbows are trying their hardest to puncture holes in my knees.

"She was just a girl that got your dick wet." He opens a filing cabinet and shuts it, looking through a folder.

"Is that what Mom was to you?"

"Boy, you better watch your tongue. Don't you talk about your mother that way! We're married, we have a family together. It's different." Still doesn't give me a passing look, his attention elsewhere.

"Before all this, at the very beginning, wasn't she just a girl from high school you got pregnant?"

"I don't know what has gotten into you and your brothers. It seems you've all lost your manners and gained a nasty case of disrespect. All you are hellbent on pissing me the hell off."

"I won't take it. I need to stay; she might need me." It's not entirely true. I need her.

"Think the best thing is for each of you to give the other space."

Space? Hadn't the past months been precisely what I wanted? Distance, freedom. But, seeing her today, she has been thriving, and I want to be a part of that success.

Right alongside her.

"Listen, son, breakups are hard. I know you're hurting. When the time is right, things will work out." His hand pats my shoulder and he gives me a soft nod.

"When Richter was five, right after Rhode was born, I left your mom. I came to the hospital drunk, saw your brothers and Rowan needing me. Man, it scared me. I had to grow some big damn balls, accepting that responsibility. The short story is, you wouldn't be here if I didn't get my act together."

"So, I should stay?"

"No, you need to figure out what you need and want, just like she has to do for herself. Can't rush the process."

"Thanks for the pep talk, Father." As I exit his office, not giving me a second look. A few of my brothers linger in the living room.

"Where's Mom?" The kitchen is bare and the stove cold, so unlike our usual routine.

"At the grocery store; she's been doing some strange stuff. Like she bought frozen burritos for us to eat. She's gone off her rocker," Ryotte calls from his spot, flipping through a comic book his sponsor sent him. The dude has been a professional skateboarder since he could walk.

"Any of you talked to Rayce?" Because he won't return my phone calls and I'm beginning to get worried.

"No, why would we? He made his choice." Richter stares at me and flexes over the counter.

"Please tell me you aren't that hardheaded? Trying to be too much like Dad, Rich."

His glare is menacing, but I don't flinch. Because fuck him and fuck my family for not accepting him any way he came.

"Watch yourself; someone might think you got some stones in your drawers." He leans back, and the challenge makes me jump to the occasion.

"Scared that I could actually take you?"

"Stop messing with each other; cut the shit already." Ranger and Razer say in unison.

"Doubt you can even reach me, little man." But before he realizes I grew six inches over summer, I take a swing and knock his ass to the ground.

"Fuck, not again." Rhode sounds exhausted from our brothers brawl.

"What is it, Richter? Are you secretly worried that the limelight will be on someone else for once? Or that Rayce coming out will look back on a second-string contender. You are due for retirement any year now." It isn't his retirement that gets me a head butt. It's the hard-glaring truth that even he wasn't good enough.

"You little fucker don't know when to shut the fuck up!" Now his elbow is jammed in my gut. I wrap an arm around his head and tighten the grip.

"No, you just don't know when to lower your pride." Somewhere I feel a warm liquid coming from my forehead.

"You are doing it wrong; got to get another angle to make him tap out." Razer comes over and watches with interest in tactics.

"Stay out of this, Raze!" My brother, whose life I have been trying to squeeze out of his body.

"Whatever, I've got to go train anyway."

"Fuck, you headed to the gym? Mind if I tag along?" Ryotte swings over the couch to head to the door.

"What, Ry? Ain't gonna stick around to see your best friend get his face smashed in?" It's Ranger who taunts him.

This makes Ryotte stop, never liking to be called out for his allegiance.

"Ugh, when am I not saving your sorry ass, River?"

"Nobody asked you, pretty boy."

"Now you went and hurt my feelings; maybe I will let him kick your ass."

Pissed off at my brothers, pissed off at my dad, pissed off at this entire fucking family. Mainly pissed at myself.

I push Richter off and shove him back down before I clock him so hard in the nose that my knuckle cracks at the same time his nose does.

"Jackpot, you cocky asshole." I flick my hand, shaking it out.

Damn, it burns.

"You okay?"

"Get the fuck off me, Ryotte. Ain't nobody needs your sympathy here." Done with this, done with them. Wherever Rayce is, I hope he has room for me.

Chapter 17

ZAILEY

"Olallie out of school or something?"

"Spring break, I think. Guess the hoes over there do extreme traveling to paradise and whatnot." Harper leans forward as she blows on the polish on her toes.

"Halo, living the good life while we are stuck in Colorado."

"Yeah, I don't know, something is off. Her energy has changed. It's like she's expecting something, coming for her. She's holding back, if that makes any sense." Leaning against her seat with her feet propped up on the dashboard.

"Did you recently accept your rule as clairvoyant? Wouldn't your mother be proud." Give her a wink as I pop my gum.

"She would, which makes me hate myself more." A slow swallow as she admits.

"Sorry, I didn't think. I know it's still a touchy subject."

"No, it's getting better. Her twins will be due any day. They seem happy, from what I've seen from a distance. Always in love, like they always have been."

"They reached out to you again?"

"Um, not really. My dad talked to me a few times, sur-face stuff. The silence almost would be better if it remained constant."

"And Amos' family?"

"They're great, amazing even. They keep hinting at us getting married. But I am unsure about the whole thing; they aren't subtle about it either." A smile grows on her face, and it seems true and real.

"What's the boyfriend say?"

"I think he wants to more out of worry he will wake up and I'll decide to be gone. Or he will turn over one night, and I've stopped breathing."

"Death still tempting?"

"Only when I feel too happy, always keeping me in check."

"He loves you."

"We never stopped."

"What's really holding you back then?"

"I'm scared if we do get married, we have kids, do the whole big shindig. We live this great, wonderful life, but one day, I'll be back facing my demons. Wondering if I can survive. I'm worried I won't want to anymore, and I will leave a mess behind. Fuck up my kids and make Shaymus hate me." A confession like that makes me realize I've struggled with this same concern.

We both think of the future, nervous there might not be a lengthy one.

"It's like when will we know we're strong enough to surpass our tragedies...?" She turns on the music and the tension of what-if fades, our voices hushing our most secret fears.

We blare the music until we hit the state line. The bass vibrating our butt cheeks with songs we know by heart.

"So, when are we going to talk about him?" Her fingers spin the volume down, and I know we are headed into another tough talk.

"Who?" Play it off like I don't know who we are talking about.

"Don't play coy; you know who I am referring to, smartass." Harper's brown hair huffs over her shoulder.

"Okay, I guess I saw this coming a few miles back. I was trying to hold off this conversation as long as I could....yeah, you could say I find your dad pretty fucking hot."

"Oh! This looks like a nice place to pull over and dump your body." She's not joking, Harper reaches over and knocks the blinker.

"Ugh...Harper, why do we have to talk about it...?" I whine more than I feel comfortable with.

"Because I know you aren't bringing it up in therapy." Those eyes look me over, daring me to deny it.

"There isn't a relationship to talk about."

"Listen, I love River. He has been moping since the breakup. He doesn't want to move out; he rarely looks like he is interested in or cares about anything."

"Are you asking me to get back together with him so you can have more alone time with Amos?"

Another look that dismantles my anger. Instead, she chooses a different approach to the conversation.

"Do you miss your mother?"

"So! River and I...I don't know if I could get over myself. Try to make things work from the opposite angle. I'm in a good place, not amped to mess that up."

"Because it would make your life difficult to trust him?"

"Harper, any time he touches me, I see his hands roaming over her. He may have taken my virginity, but he slept with her first. It's hard to look past. I feel bad, it feels like I blame him, but there isn't more to say." A shrug worms through my shoulders.

"Maybe you should stop comparing yourself to her for not being who she was."

"She was a monster. I don't want to be like her."

"I meant who she was to River in your mind. Obviously, you've built her up to be something, she might not even be to him. We don't get second chances on introductions. We barely get chances at anything new as it is. Want to know a fun tidbit?" She nudges me a bit, giving me a pleasant wide smile.

"Shoot it to me."

"Zailey Jensen is stronger than her."

"Well, that's not hard; she is dead." I flip the visor down and look at my lips as I pout.

"Not seeing the bigger picture here, sweetie."

"Enlighten me."

"She wasn't brave enough to face the consequences of what she did. You not only recovered, but stood tall when everyone called you a fraud. People like her are weak; they prey on the strong, hoping they can steal your power."

"She did steal it."

"But she can't anymore." We hold hands for a few minutes letting the weight of the truth lift off of my shoulders.

Chapter 18

RIVER

"God, you sure know how to bring the mood down, River." My brother Richter smacks the back of my head, putting a drink in my hand.

"Can somebody get this man a lap dance?" Rhode shouts out to a few strippers waltzing around in pasties and thongs.

"What are you even doing here? Pretty sure your ass is underage, buddy."

"Ranger said it was cool." He knocks my knees, hoping I shift over on the couch.

"Where are Rayce and Ryder?"

"Those two will come on Saturday. They have finals or some assignment due."

"Are you not a slave to college work also?" My head rolls back and forth on the edge of the sofa.

"Actually, I fast-tracked and am going to be starting my master's program in the fall in Colorado Springs."

"Why are you always trying to outshine me?"

"Not hard, barely even have to try."

Lunge over him as I wrap my arm around his head.

"Take it back, rowdy Rhode!" I tickle his side, and he lets out a high pitched giggle. "Aw, still have a girly laugh, my little brother. Guess it's all you got since your balls haven't dropped yet." I slowly release him, but he is quick. When he straightens, his hand slaps my nuts so hard I feel like my whole body vibrates from the hit.

"Ugh, you mother fucker." He's halfway across the club now, scared I'll beat his bony ass. Fuck, I crumble to the dirty floor, hoping I don't contract some type of STD while I'm down here holding onto my manhood.

"Rhode get you good?" Amos finds a seat a few feet away; he laughs, emptying another beer bottle.

"Gotta slow down before coach makes you run ladders."

"Season is almost over, spring training down the road." The waitress brings him two others; he places one next to my head.

"Thanks." Push up on my knees, slumping back to my spot on the couch.

"No problem, you know I've always got your back." Our eyes trailed the room, our brothers hanging, having a good time.

"Nice of your brothers to come. Damn, Fowler sprouted up like a weed. Dude is almost taller than me." River mentions them as they interact with his brothers.

"Yep, Rourke is still an asshole, it seems."

"Doesn't have it in him to be anything less than a son of a bitch. Wonder what they will when they must throw in their jerseys. If they are hard to handle now, who the fuck knows how they will be after."

A show begins, and the lights go down. We spend the night roaming the strip, the street filled with views and good times.

"What do you think the girls are doing right now?"

"From what I've heard, Olallie is sixteen, still in high school. Maybe they went cow tipping? Who knows what happens in Oklahoma? Probably bored out of their minds." Amos looks calm; inside I know he is a mess of worry.

Both of us trying not to stare at our phones, hoping there will be messages from one of the girls.

"Well, dickweeds, shall we see who can score the most cash at the end of the night? Up in the suite, any takers?" Razer beckons us all back to the hotel. But we wave him off, staying a while longer at the club.

"Ranger, tell us how you purposed. Go on, we are all gushing at the seams, gushing over every detail." Razer hoots, and we all follow in a holler.

"It was a dark and cold night..."

Alarms start blaring, and the main attraction steps out on stage and I kid you not, I think every one of our sorry asses falls in love with her.

"We have quite the treat for you tonight, gentleman. One of our veterans has come home for a visit. And she sure likes to meet new friends. Give it up for the one and only Cashmere!" The announcer sounds like a seedy freak.

Not platinum blonde, this woman has a wave of fire hair tinted by the Gods themselves. Her skin glows so smooth, it sparks the spotlight.

"Holy shit!"

"Smoking hot."

"You've got to be shitting me." Rhode stands and makes his way to the edge of the stage.

"Whoa, little Cody, there's a line. You can't be there." Ranger shouts at him to come back to the booths.

"Jayden?" Rhode is about to scale the stage when a bodyguard stops him. It's the first time I see my brother actively get violent.

"Oh shit! Rhode, this isn't what it looks like; it was a one-time thing." Cashmere, or whoever the hell the strip-per on prime time is, stops her splits and goes to the edge.

"Damn, things just got interesting." Richter pipes up like a bitch in heat for some drama.

"Don't touch me; get your goddamn hands off me, you motherfuckers!" We're all shocked by the caveman that is crawling out of Rhode.

Guess nobody can tame the Hendrix fever like we initially thought. Everyone waiting for the steam to escalate, and then boom goes the dynamite.

He is shoving these men who could easily knock his ass out cold.

"Let him go! Let him go! He's my boyfriend, for god's sake!" Cashmere clamors in thick high heels, begging the bodyguards to let our brother go.

But it won't be that easy, especially when Razer gets up and starts laughing at them. Then Ranger must show who has the biggest dick, and of course, Richter needs a pat on the back.

"At your grandmother's house for the weekend, huh? For the love of Rowan's God, how goddamn stupid do you think I am?" Rhode points and yells as the guards try to restrain him.

Chaos breaks loose.

Ryotte somehow is on one of the goons' back. Razer has some guy, another customer in a headlock. Ranger is playing tug-o-war with his drink. Amos just stares at all of them, witnessing the testosterone.

"So much for forever, huh, Jayden?" He pulls out a ring box and pushes it into her hands. Her mouth gapes open.

"It's the one you designed from the meteor rock, oh my god, Rhode. It's beautiful." The model we were all drooling over breaks her act and flutters her eyes with emotion.

"Well, it's all yours. Hope one day you can use it on some sucker who deserves you."

Oh, shit, not him, too, locked in the cycle of promise.

"Guess your victory is knowing I could be fooled; I wonder, though, to what degree. Lucky for me, right place, right time. Have good rest of your semester Miss Cashmere." Dude has some big swinging gonads, not even trying to make her feel bad. All he does is put his fists in his dress pants and turns with his head down and walk away.

"Rhode! Rhode! Wait, please let me explain!" She tries to move through us, but obviously, that's impossible.

"Sorry, darlin', seems like he doesn't want anything to do with you." Richter leans against the stage, arms folded like he is the ruler.

"And who the fuck are you guys? His friends. Though I haven't seen you boys, around campus." Her tears blink away quickly, putting on a neutral face.

"Nah, sweet girl. We're his brothers; nice meeting you, by the way." I loop my arm around her shoulders.

"Oh, shit." Lightbulb.

Chapter 19

ZAILEY

"Harper, tell me we are looking at the same fine specimens of mankind." Zailey pushes her sunglasses to the top of her head.

We arrived a few moments ago, and the driveway is extensive. The home itself makes me flinch and cower.

A parade of beautifully tanned men lines muscle cars and trucks.

"Careful, these boys have records." Calhoun, who happens to be Olallie's half-brother, grabs our bags from the car and carries them inside.

"Like criminal or juvie? I'm excellent with either!" She hollers after him.

Olallie stands beside us, watching the guys check things underneath the engines.

Ladies, I've missed you. These are the Sonny boys.

"Which piece of meat is taking a long way home after leaving you at night, if you know what I mean?" Zailey's hand coasts through a wave.

The blue-eyed girl rolls her eyes and starts to point and spell. The first guy her eyes linger on has us all taking a step back.

His shoulders massive, his face pierced with the tendencies of a hard motherfucker. But damn if we don't take a minute to quiver at the clench of his jaw. The smolder that is sucked into the darkness of his eyes.

Lawson, and that's his best friend Verse.

"Hellloooo, Verse." The smooth drawl grows seduction until the end. It doesn't help that she is right. Verse is a lengthy fool who has that Asian persuasion going on.

"God, Zailey, keep it dry."

Vayden, Verse's little brother, is my friend.

"Don't look too little to me, honey."

"Food, can we go eat some? Before, I literally throw up all over your paved stone driveway." I make the action of throwing up more dramatic.

"Did she say brothers? Hey! Have you guys ever, tag-teamed?" Zailey elbows my side, offering me in on some action.

"What the actual fuck? You are disgusting!" It's her coping mechanism, I know this, but I still can't hold back from giving her grief.

"Just because you've settled on riding one stick for the foreseeable future doesn't mean I have to be confined to missionary thoughts." Giving us an eyeful as she licks her lips.

"Verse? Did you say his name was? If you happen to like being tied up and having your dignity stripped, Zailey here is your girl."

"I could get into that." Verse, who try as I might not to, when I stare, it's hard to look away. Don't know what they are doing down here in Oklahoma, but they are doing it right.

"See no harm in flirting; the universe doesn't know what I want until I ask." This better not be a foretelling of how this trip is going to go, because she on the hunt could not be less than exhausting.

"Is this the famous Stormy in the flesh? She is quite feisty." The man ropes his arms around Olallie's waist.

"The one and only, but the rest of the men I play with call me danger." She winks at Verse.

"I hope the holy one swallows you up for that one, you compulsive slut." I grab her hand and drag her to the car. Forcing the charade to stop before I cut her tongue out.

We all squish into a booth at the local diner. Fried goodies arrive, and the boys dig.

"So...Lawson, where did you find our sweet innocent Olallie? Was it on the playground? She's only fourteen years old, you know, don't be tricked." I sit in between Vayden and one of Lawson's cousins.

Olallie grabs a ton of greasy fries and chucks them at Zailey's face.

"I wouldn't say she has much innocence left." Lawson coughs into his shoulder, and fist bumps Verse.

"Showing your age, gentlemen." The one comment I made during lunch.

"Oh, dirty girl! Have you popped her cherry vessel? Has your petal been plucked? When did this happen? Wait, don't tell me, was it in the locker room? Or under the moonlight on her balcony?"

Vayden leans closer to me as he whispers, "Girl never stops talking, does she?"

"Just wait until you get her drunk, she becomes philosophical. Wait, I forget you all are underage. None of you even know what alcohol tastes like, right?" Shove a nudge into his shoulder.

Silence covers the crowd until Olallie squirts root beer out of her nose.

"Oh, Jesus!" Verse scatters away, on top of someone else's lap.

We all hear the quiet whisper, low and steady of, "*Fuck it burns.*"

"That's what she said!"

"Vayden!" Zailey chastises him.

"Sorry, I hate myself for it. But damn it was going to happen one way or another."

"Damn, baby. That was some extremist range." The table literally vibrates with laughter, and I take this moment to look around and feel so grateful to be a part of this moment.

We all laugh until tears form in our eyes.

"Where are we headed tonight?"

"We've got a surprise for you girls." Olallie's sweetheart has a sweet voice. I wonder if she ever rests her head on his chest and lets that feeling rumble down to the core.

"Great, we're breaking someone out of jail again." Vayden's shoulders dip down.

"Again? Man, Harper, I think we are missing out on some fun times here. Maybe we need to relocate to a new environment." Eyes shine bright with hope, too eager for the change.

"We are not moving out to Oklahoma. No offense."

"None taken, you've got to have thick blood to survive out here." A wink reaches over to me from Verse.

"Don't taunt her; she knows the degrees hell truly burns, my friend."

"What will you do without your beloved marijuana? It's only medical here."

"I could get a prescription."

"Because you get along with doctors so well."

"Enough of this banter. It's getting dark, so let's move out." A spark from Verse's lips lets loose.

"Do we need to change?"

"Got anything shorter that shows off your ass?" He winks, and I can only imagine this ending very badly.

"I think I do, let me look in my bag; here it is, Verse." She flips him the bird.

"Oh, sour attitude. Won't be getting you the good weed I bought for this joyous occasion."

"What flavor? Give it to me!"

"Only for a kiss?"

"Where?" Literally taking the bait, to do what she has to in order to get her buzz.

"God, you are hopeless!" My head tips back to let the children fight over their consumption.

From the corner of my eye, I see Olallie's hands start to move.

I can smell it from here.

"What? I can't even smell it, baby." A big whiff, Lawson tries to inhale the scent.

When I lock eyes with Olallie, she shrugs, but there is something else. And I can't look away.

"O? Olallie?" A few tugs to her hair and the connection is broken. She blinks away a message I spend most of the night deciphering.

When we walk into this place, it looks like an old train station. *Hudson's Hook* flushes with a marquee sign.

"This is your cousin's place?" Those two have been joined at the hip; Verse and Zailey perfectly balance out each other.

"No, this is Lawson's cousin. Most of his cousins are the Sonny boys." Verse shouts back to her.

Music is blaring when I look around. Everybody is carefree for having a good time. The vibe is beginning to affect me.

"Sonny boys?" Only Z would need to know all the specific details of a stranger's life.

"Hudson, Lawson, most of the guys have a son on the end of their names. Except his little sister, Crimsyn. We call her sin. It all started with his oldest cousin Dawson; he's been in lock up for a couple years now. But, there are about ten to twenty of them in sum."

"Small town trends?"

"You have no idea."

But I did because I'd come from the close-knit community. One that now reflects the perception of others over actual events.

We dance, and I feel the music in every part of my body. Zailey shifts around Verse while Vayden sidesteps by me, making sure no one comes close enough to touch me.

Olallie is lost in Lawson's arms, slow dancing. They hover around each other, and the way makes me want to move in the same direction.

Bodies move, and I've never felt so alive. It feels good, embracing how unrestricted it is to belong here. Where no one knows you or expects anything from you.

But I stop when I sense another feeling rise.

"What's wrong, Harp?" Her arms are above her head as she moves side to side in front of Verse.

"I feel so turned on right now."

"Of course you do; I wonder what Amos would think?" I see her mouth smile, but I don't hear the giggle.

"He would love it, I should tell him. Do you feel this good? It's amazing."

"Oh, shit, Harper, where did my drink go?"

"The water? I finished it; this music, it's like it's in my soul!"

"Don't get pissed, pretty girl."

"Never." My best friend moves the hair away from my face and brings my face really close to hers. Almost close enough to kiss.

"You are high; my drink had a little dose of ecstasy in it."

"Really?" I beam with such excitement.

"Yes, shit, I am so sorry. Do you want to leave? Sleep it off?"

"Is this what drugs always feel like?"

"Most of them."

"This is incredible, let's stay here forever and dance."

A few more hours go by, and my cheeks hurt from the increase of smiles, ones I rarely allow to cross my face.

Let's head back to my house.

Our little friend who seems more mature than any of us combined maneuvers her fingers to gather us up to vacate.

Wait! I've got to use the restroom.

"I'll go with her, might as well release the dam."

Laughing, it's the only thing that comes out of my mouth. "Oh my God, have you always been this funny?"

"You don't think I'm funny when you're not high."

"Oh, my goodness, I should. You are hilarious. Ow! My sides hurt." Leaning to one side as the humor starts to turn into pain.

"I'll take her to the car. Come on, silly girl let's find our way." My bodyguard for the night wrestles me to the front door.

"I've only had sex with two people."

"Well, I hate to break the news, but I'm still in high school." His hands go up defensive like I might strip him naked in the parking lot.

My high must be wearing off.

"Olallie is special, like unearthly. Do you feel weird when you're around her?"

"Yes, I thought it was a fluke, but she dismantled my walls like she invented the A-bomb."

"It's creepy."

"It's a gift." Vayden's voice hitches a bit, and I wonder what glorious secret pain Olallie stole from him.

"Give me a minute, I've got to make a phone call." Tap my pockets until I find my phone.

"Harper, hello?" Shaymus' voice comes through loud on speaker. A song in the background has my hips swinging again.

"SHAYMUS! It's me! Harper!"

"I know, my Calico girl, why are you yelling?" A chuckle from his throat meets my ears.

"Did you know I've only had sex with two people?"

"Yes? I do know that…"

"Vayden thinks I am trying to jump him into submission. He's still in high school. I wasn't trying to get on him at all. I have you."

"Yes, you do."

"See, you are all I need. Hey, have you ever wondered how the stars glow? Like do they take turns, is there an off switch?"

"Harper, are you drunk?"

"High…hold on one second. Vayden, what did Zailey say she spiked the drink with?"

"Ecstasy."

"Someone spiked your drink with ecstasy?"

"Zailey gave me water. It was good water. Why doesn't everyone feel this good all the time?"

"Calico, are you safe? Who are you with? Where is Zailey?" His voice is dangerous, which makes me laugh a little.

"She went to the bathroom with Olallie."

"Vayden! Quick we need help; it's Olallie! Find Calhoun ASAP, man. Kalonie and her goons did something." Verse yells from the second floor window.

"Oh shit! Harper, come on." Vayden drags me toward the warehouse before I know what's happened.

"Oh, I've got to go."

"Somebody call an ambulance!"

"Harper? Harper! Is everything okay?" Shaymus yells at me, wanting an answer. But I drop the call and rush into the building as everyone seems unaware that my friends are in trouble.

Chapter 20

RIVER

"What'd she say?" I know I'm as eager as a toddler.

"I—I think there is some sort of trouble. She wasn't making much sense. Zailey slipped her some ecstasy, and something happened to their friend they're visiting." He runs a hand through his hair. His eyes go to our brothers, and I look over my shoulder for a second, but I come back to his face.

"Well?"

"Listen, I think I should go and make sure they're okay." Amos moves quick, grabbing his wallet.

"Let's go!" My anxious temper grows with each step, and he seems to regress.

"Are you sure you should be coming?" The peak from his brown eyes makes me question my position.

"Even if it wasn't for Zailey, Amos, I've got your back. I'm coming for both of you."

"Yeah, thanks, man."

We don't say it, but we question the possibility of finding them worse than when we waved goodbye to them. In our parking lot, it was a careful farewell. One brought on by submissive feelings, and I worry I won't ever love another human being the same way. Zailey causes destruction, a warpath of the inevitable.

All I can guess is that we were the only ones left standing to wait for the world around us to stop shaking, giving us a chance to breathe.

"I'm going to ask Harper to marry me." Amos sits in the aisle seat as I adjust my seatbelt, looking out onto the runway.

Marriage? A few moments go by, and I have to contemplate the obvious, not the complications in friendship, but the realm of the possibility of having that with someone, mainly Zailey.

"Marriage? Like a whole ceremony, rings, and dresses?" The trouble I am having is not seeing it. The problem is I see mine and Z's more evident than theirs.

Flashes of smiles, intimate conversations, and love I have waited years to make final.

"Yes, I think—well, I think we are ready for that next step, and I wanted to ask you since you've been here with us through everything. Will you be my best man, River?" This is how Shaymus Griffin does things, he asks with eyes straightforward, avoiding the struggle to be emotional.

"Of course, dude. As long as you are mine in return." I shake my head up and down, saying yes. I'm deciding right now that our friendship has been through so many downfalls. It has made me grateful for the moments of peace.

"Do you think she'll say yes? What am I saying, she has to. We have a bond that is scorched into stone. Not even the heavens could tear us apart."

Give him a small nod as I rearrange my long legs to get more comfortable. There has to be some connection that holds strength from that type of source.

"Zailey." On the edge of my voice breaking, blinking away the possibilities.

"Hey, man, I'm sure they are okay. Harper hasn't texted me back. I'm sure when we land, they will have an update. No sense in worrying about it right now, before we know anything." A good speech that was made to comfort both of us.

"Yeah, I just, sometimes with the girls. With what they've been through, I worry if I say one thing, then a bomb drops on their dignity. They've changed. And if you don't adjust or gain some gonads, you're going to lose her."

"I know what you mean..." Maybe he is reliving finding Harper on his front lawn.

"I don't know if an action or a phrase is a trigger. For the longest time, I was stressed out, walking on eggshells. Hoping like fuck I didn't do anything wrong. But I think the more I treated her like she was seconds away from breaking, the more she didn't need me to be strong." My fingerprints pinch the bridge of my nose, finding relief.

"Things are different now; they've changed, man. Being intimate with her is on another spectrum. Before, it was all quick and tender. Now it's a slow burn that is rough and sometimes aggressive."

I try to think about being intimate with Zailey, and there isn't much I can compare. Our first time a few weeks after Sawyer's accident. Then some casual fooling around, but we've yet to mend the bridge from mind-blowing sex to actual love making.

"I was scared to touch her. When we lived together for those months at the beginning of the year. Every time I got turned on, I couldn't get the image of someone else's hands on her body. As if the marks would be a physical reminder."

"From her sleeping with your brother? Ryder? Dude, you literally slept with more women than I remember."

"Not him."

"Well, who then?"

"What happened between Sawyer and her makes me sick. I feel like a goddamn pussy. If I was more aware, maybe I would have noticed?"

"Noticed your girlfriend was molesting her best friend?"

"Dude, quiet down with that shit! Someone might hear you." My head snaps around to see if anyone is listening to us. We are busting each other's bubbles at this point.

"Why? Do you think her actions reflect badly on you? Are you somehow held accountable for what Sawyer's twisted intentions were? Because you should think about that; you should face what it meant, not to you but to her. At the end of the fucking day, River, you didn't get betrayed by people who you thought loved you. Zailey did, she did for years, being manipulated. Then for you, her parents openly accuse her of lying. Her mom died, and you literally abandoned her when she needed you most."

And there goes the detonator.

"Think about how that made her feel because I can tell you that there isn't a morning I don't wake up still panicked that I left Harper to die."

"She won't forgive me for not sticking by her side. Fuck, I feel like a damn fool. Jesus, I've been an idiot. Making the situation about me. How I am going to cope with a woman who was abused and probably has PTSD?" Fuck, I punch the seat in front of me, forgetting we aren't alone on this plane ride. "Shit, sorry." But Amos stares at me, finally seeing what I'm made of, and I take a rule out of his book.

He doesn't apologize for who he is; he gladly stands in front of the firing squad waiting to be relieved of his consequences.

"She might not forgive me." A bite on my bottom lip pinches deep under my teeth.

"I think their version of forgiveness is a different transition than how we normal people function."

"What do you mean, Amos?"

"Why did Harper forgive me? Has she fully committed to me staying? Or in the back of her mind, is she just biding her time until I decide to leave again?"

"Where are you going with this?" Itching the side of my head while we continue.

"It's something I noticed the other day when we were lying in bed. She said something that rubbed me the wrong way."

"What did Harper say?"

"River, I think people like Harper, like Zailey, realize how fragile life can be. How easy it is to be caught inside the dilemma, reliving the tragedy like that's all they have to offer is a state of suffering." He fixes the sleeves on his shirt, pulling down the cuffs.

Covering the indiscreet black ink that wraps around his wrists. Chained to the past, a reminder of the sacrifices we endure to give up our most precious obsessions.

We are both selfish, accepting reprimanding. Sins soon were the one thing that covered our hands, always dried with blood. There wasn't a task of needing to be spot-free with our women by our sides. Each of us accepting the others with grace.

Chapter 21

ZAILEY

Outside of Olallie's house, I sit on a stump. Down the hill a few hundred yards, the wire fence separates an inmate fortress and the power-hungry.

At the base of the tree, I flex my foot out, noticing my hand is bruised.

"Fuck…" Fingers barely straighten, I flinch them back into a fist.

"Wild night." Verse comes to stand next to me. I barely give him a glance with the pounding in my head.

All I can do is nod.

Red marks circle my wrists where the handcuffs locked my consequences.

"Zailey, what you did last night for Olallie, for my brother."

"Don't make me into some hero."

"It means something, Z. You've got a good heart." His arms are folded, and shades hang over his eyes.

"Your pops in there?"

"Nah, mine is a good working citizen. Now Lawson's daddy, he is in maximum. Might be as bad as death row."

The facts don't shock me; they were ruined by my stint in a cell. It was something to shake our heads.

"Being loyal is a fault of mine."

"Nah, girl, those actions last night is what defines you. Distinguishes you between the scared bitches and those who were brave enough to stand up."

"Dude, I got arrested. As in violent crime, in front of your eyes."

The teenage boy beside me shrugs like getting arrested in this town isn't a big deal.

"What, the badass girl doesn't want a bad rap sheet?"

"Not funny, high school sweetheart."

Verse throat chuckles as an arm is thrown around my shoulders.

"He'll wipe your slate clean, little birdie."

"Who? Olallie's dad?"

"No, keep up. Lawson's stepdad, Patch." I believe he is referring to the deputy who met us at the station.

A wind picked up, traveling through the trees. My eyes draw close, trying to remember what this place feels like.

"You okay? What a sad face you've got."

"Yeah, ha, just back home. There's a lot of history; it's hard to confront."

"Come live with me, kitty cat."

"Please, what are you seventeen? Still in grade school, little lover."

"So, there's a two, three year gap. I've fucked older women than that, princess."

"First of all, those poor women. Second, the minute you turn eighteen, I will overlook the number, and we can bang out our differences."

"Promise?"

Promise. Promise? Promise me always, forever, for now. But still, always remember to never promise us an ending.

"Z?" Speak of the devil who whispers in my ear.

"Huh?"

"Listen, bro, you better let me get through." But I know it can't be his voice, why would he be here.

"Ain't nobody here your bro." Vayden's voice comes on full strength."

"Who the fuck is that?"

"River?"

"Want to take a few steps away from my girlfriend, little man?"

"Little man? Who you calling that? Oh my gosh, Z, do you know this guy? Dude, you know you're like an inch or so taller than me. Maybe fifty pounds less."

"Watch it! I don't know how you gentlemen do things down here. But in good ol' Colorado, my brothers and I aren't scared to throw down." River puffs out his chest like a cartoon character.

Verse and Vayden hold back a laugh, hoping our Colorado boys push them a little further.

"Throwdown? What were you raised in the '90s?"

"What are you doing here, River? Fuck, no, no! Has Amos come to claim my Harper?" I storm passed both men on a rampage to find some clarity. "Damnit, Harper, we have one more week!"

"Don't look at me, I didn't demand his ass to come to swoop down here." She looks just as pissed as I feel.

"We're fine, everything is fine."

"You got arrested for assault." Amos and his big mouth have to speak out about anything of his choosing.

"Shut the fuck up, Amos! God, it's like you never stop opening that trap of yours. Let the adults talk. Harper, please, for the love of your mother's angels, make him go home."

"The college won't let you go back there with probation on your name." River tries to speak reason with me.

"The college? River, I dropped out after we got back from the cabin."

"Explains why the school said you were inactive." He shrugs like he already checked up on me.

"It was all too much, you and school. I—I couldn't do any of it anymore. I'm not made for certain things."

"Zailey, what are you talking about? We will go back to Denver. We'll get you signed up for classes. Find a different job, I'll move back in with you to help out." River is in my face, throwing situations left and right.

His words blend as much as I blink. I shake my head, trying to tell him to stop.

"Zailey? Hey, it's okay, look at me." Harper tries to soothe me, but her voice is blurry.

A quick breath in and out again. Maybe too quickly, because I try to gain more and it's no there.

My knees buckle, and the bright sky turns to the only shade I know.

Black.

Chapter 22

RIVER

"What the fuck happened?" Voices start to shout out worry.

"Dude, is she unconscious?" Obviously, motherfucker.

"Get away from her!" I try to shove the other guys away.

"Everybody back the hell up!" Harper's voice demands things, but I can't think straight.

"Z? Zailey? Are you okay, baby?" The limp woman in my arms doesn't stir. I look at her face, and black smudges drip from her eyes. "Harp? Oh my, God Harper, is she crying? Is she hurt? Help me help her. Make it stop. Make it stop."

"River, man, set her down. You've got to calm down." Amos pulls me back.

"I was just trying to help; she needs help. Please, I can help her." I plead with anyone that will listen.

"Where's Olallie?" This time, Harper's voice isn't commanding. Instead, it's a worry.

"Out front, I'll grab her." Vayden jumps and hauls ass. I'm on my knees, trying to figure out what I did wrong. How I continue to do everything wrong, it seems.

"Shit! She's seizing! Damn it, ugh, shit, shit, shit!"

"Hold on, I'll call my sister. We live down the road." Verse I think says it.

"No, Leonie's in the house. She'll be out in a minute." The small blonde girl's boyfriend speaks for her.

A girl with a simple face and short brown hair makes her way over to us. She looks around once and then puts Zailey on her side, pries open her mouth, and shoves an apple inside.

"She'll choke!"

"She'll bite her tongue off. Stress-induced seizures. Olallie says she has medication?" All she does is put out a hand. Harper places a couple pills in it. Watching her friend slowly stop shaking.

"There we go, it's almost over."

"Does she have a concussion?"

"Did she hit her head?"

"No."

"Then, no. Do you not understand how injuries to the brain work? Do you need a demonstration?"

Olallie puts a hand in the air, flicks her hand out, under her chin.

"You're welcome." Leonie, I think we just met, leaves without looking back.

"Is she going to be okay? Should we get her into the house?" I don't loosen my grip on her body. Knowing that I may have caused this attack makes me even more nervous.

"Sure, River. Follow Olallie inside. She's going to be fine, just a little overwhelmed is all." Harper pats my shoulder as we walk toward the house.

Let me get us some drinks. Olallie signs the words, still coming down from the excitement.

"O, let me get them. Your hands, remember?" Lawson bends his head and kisses the top.

Her palms still wrapped with gauze and bandages.

"What happened last night?" Amos tilts his head to Olallie's hands.

"She has an evil stepsister." Is all Harper gives us before Olallie angles her head, tapping her wrists?

"Half-sister, same thing."

"Your sister did this to you?" Well, I guess the world isn't as shiny as I first believed it to be.

"She's been bullying her, but it's more hazing than casual," Vayden speaks from the corner, a book in his hand.

"And you guys weren't there to protect her, some friends."

"Shaymus..." Harper tries to butt in, but it's no use. Emotions are running hot; the tension is cutthroat.

"What do you think we do with our women exactly? You think you're any better than the rest of us? The stories I hear about the two of you assholes, I look like a damn saint." A few glasses break when Lawson makes his way through the kitchen doors.

"Law, maybe we should cool off. Let's take it outside, go for a drive." His best friend heads his way; Olallie scurries out of the room.

"Maybe you should listen to your pal there?" Amos stands rolls back his shoulders, ready for a fight.

Olallie comes back with a broom and a dustpan. Harper takes them from her and gets down on her knees.

"What are you doing? Now isn't the time to defend your pride." My eyes go to Zailey, who is still wiped out.

"Maybe you should listen to your pal." Lawson stands a few feet away. I can imagine how this plays out.

Amos bumps chests with Lawson, they throw punches, then Verse and I step in to break it up. We start tumbling, Harper starts cussing at Amos, Olallie sits in the corner, continues to try and clean with her damaged hands.

We leave with our tails tucked between our legs.

"Think this through, it's not worth it." My hands are up, trying to smooth the situation over.

A few seconds from losing control, and we all let our shoulders drop.

Lawson breathes, and his fists let go of the hold. "Shit, O. Hey, baby girl, I'll clean it up." He tries to go near her, but her fingers point at different angles.

She drops her hands, the wet bandages slipping off. Revealing blisters that look like acid was poured on them.

"O, shit, they're bleeding. Hey, we need to cover those cuts. Are you in pain?" Lawson moves to go near her, but she raises the bloody palms at him.

The liquid runs down her arms. Her eyes speak, and Lawson stops in his tracks.

"Vayden, help her while I take him out back for a smoke." Verse steers Lawson to the backyard.

"Olallie, come on, careless girl. Let's get your mess under control." He cradles her into the kitchen.

"Isn't it a great feeling being so powerful, having everyone bow down to your tantrums?" A few clinks of shards of glass make it into the pile next to Harper's hands.

"I should have shut up." Already hanging his head.

"Shit!" A finger skims the edge of the broken glass. "River, down the third hallway door on the left. It's Olallie's room; I am sure Zailey would be much more comfortable waking up there." Harper motions for me to move her out of the room.

My arms go under her, lifting her to my body.

"I wonder what a trip would have been like without having my boyfriend come in and turn it into his show. Guess we will never know will we Shaymus?"

"You're mad at me because I care about you?"

"No, honey, I am irate. Because you're suffocating with these decisions you make on my behalf. It isn't your care; it's the need to be in control."

"Control? If I had any control, I wouldn't have allowed this bullshit trip with your friend who drugs you." I can hear his feet stomp around as I make my way down the hall.

"Zailey, that friend you just can't seem to accept was one of the few people who decided I was worth their time."

"Do I not do that for you every day? Am I not the first person that wakes up grateful that you are alive?"

"It could just be guilt."

"Don't say that, we are far past that stage in our relationship."

"What relationship exactly? The fairytale one you hope will happen, or the reality where things are actually true?"

"Harper, marry me."

"So we're going with the fairytale one. In that case, how can I say no?"

"Well, don't sound so excited."

Why in the hell is this hallway so long?

"Shaymus, I hope you know how lucky you are to have River. Because it is mind-blowing how much people don't like you."

"I don't need people to like me."

"It's not lonely on the top of your pedestal?" Her voice gets a little more agitated, and I'm sure she doesn't notice the pain as the tiny shards meet her clear skin.

"The only person I have ever needed is myself."

"No sentence has ever been truer."

"Fuck, Harper, give me a goddamn break. You know I didn't mean it like that; we just got engaged, doesn't that count for anything?"

I finally make it to the bedroom; I close the door with force. Set Zailey on the bed and sit across the room. The room is extensive, a tall ceiling, a patio out the side.

Not tempted to look in the bathroom or closet. My phone buzzes a message from a girl whose name is saved as 3x.

Guess the sex was good...thinking of a reply when Zailey lets out a worried whimper.

The reality, here it is. I did this.

"Zailey? Baby, are you okay?" Nearly crawling to the bedside, on my knees praying to momma's God that she'll be good as new. "I'm sorry, I really am. It's probably a phrase you don't hear often coming out of my lips." A poor excuse for a laugh lingers on my lips.

"Do you remember that Halloween party we went to at Lox Rutledge's house?" Images flash over my memory; I avoid the ones where she isn't the main attraction. "We danced all night; Sawyer was sitting glaring at us. But she wasn't having any fun that night. After a while, I forgot we were egging her on. I got lost in touching you, the way my hands roamed your body. How nice you fit pressed against me."

A bird knocks its beak on the window a few times before it flies away.

"Zailey, I know I fucked up. Not as bad as my buddy Amos is doing right now with Harper, but close. I need you to wake up, open those gorgeous eyes, and tell me to go home." Seconds pass, and I wait for the indefinite timeline that would make my hope worth something.

"You were right about my dad. What happened with Rayce, we should have all been by his side. I couldn't go on that internship. I'm too weak to leave my family. It depends too much on the noise to live somewhere too quiet. Does that make sense? Who knows, maybe I should still go." She resists the urge to stir, and I turn and plop down on my rear end.

"I keep thinking about what would happen if I went and never came back. What a life without any of the Hendrix brothers breathing down my back would be like. A life where the name Sawyer wasn't tied to me. Where my heart wouldn't belong to yours."

Being someone else could be easy, might be freeing. I wonder if that's how Zailey feels, always in pursuit of becoming a new version of herself.

"She was wrong, you know. Sawyer said you weren't strong enough to fall in love, which is why you never had before. But you were already buried deep. I found out how brilliant and daring it was swimming out past the safe harbor. When she just showed me the shore." I squint my eyes tight, trying to make the tears go someplace else.

"It's always been you, Z. It will always be you for me. And until you realize the same, I'll wait. Be patient, be understanding, because I realize that's all you've asked of me to give to you."

I'll tell you I love you every day until the day I die.

Chapter 23

ZAILEY

A few months ago, I blinked open to a starry night swirled on the vaulted ceiling. I tried not to think where I was. If I had met my end and the words I should have said to those that loved me most.

In those seconds, I found solitude; it was almost peaceful, the warmth coming through the window. Odd morning sunlight made me sit still and not stir in my surroundings.

Maybe I was meeting my conclusion. It had passed, and there I was awaiting sentencing I didn't even fear anymore.

Finally, it was over.

The drenched worry, an endless fear of having to be accepted. I knew now I didn't have to be. Relief scattered over my body, and I felt the rushing sensation ease my soul. Just like my old friend Mary Jane use to do.

Aw, the need for a good blunt was miles away. I was desperate to stay catatonic right here, giving in to the abyss. Right now, finally, I was free, all the folklore of the afterlife, and it was final.

I would release a breath of air, but I know none would expel. And the idea makes me smile. Making me blink once more, hoping the sensation never wears thin.

No more struggle to survive, to beat the non-sense that kept my confidence hostage.

"Hey, her eyes are open. She's awake." A male voice rings into my eardrums, and the sound triggers too loudly.

Careful to turn my head to the left, where he leans over, River.

"No." Adjusting my head back on the pillow, closing my eyes before forcing them again open. "No." Panic wasn't shifting my perspective.

"Zailey?"

"What are you doing here?" At a loss, my freedom screeching as it was dragged away.

A once beautiful face I use to dream about falls in defeat. "Don't you remember? Amos and I came to make sure you're okay." His fingers reach and intertwine with mine.

I don't mean to, but emptiness replaces the affection I have for him. Pulling my palm away to let it lay flat on my stomach.

The breath I was holding is let out; a profoundly disappointed sigh echoes the room as I sit up and lean against the wall.

River's hand holds still on my knee, his gracious fresh pine eyes pleading with a lost cause.

"Harper, they want us to leave?" I look at the door, where she stands timid, like Olallie's usual demeanor.

Ready for me to rebel against the request. But she nods, giving me a sympathetic smile.

"Well, let's go." Make my way to the front door, I see my bag already packed. They've made the decision for me.

The whole way home is tunnel vision. These people try to talk to me, and I remember nodding here and there, not meeting eyes.

They're worried about me, they stare at me, and I want to close my eyes and vanish.

"You going to tell me what's going on with you? Ever since we got back from Oklahoma, you've been in a fog. Are you taking your medications?" Harper lays on my bed as I sit next to her on the floor.

"Yes, I have been." I have actually been consistent with dosages, doctor visits, and groups.

"So, what is it...?" I look over my shoulder, wondering if she cares, or if River has pressured her into asking.

"When I woke up on Olallie's bed, I thought I died. Not that I had gone to heaven, but I was finally done having to be here." Lines on my arms remind me of a teenage girl who thought the end was far closer than the healing.

A few moments go by, and she finally speaks. "What was it like?" The hushed need in her voice makes me know we're still the same suffering girls we once were.

"It felt...it felt free."

"It's—It's hard not to want that." Her voice begs a similar escape.

We both flirt with the fantasy of being unconfined. Our depths of self-hate ruined with hope. Each uplifting phrase is dedicated to making us try one more day.

And we do, again and again.

We keep trying and shifting our views on possibilities. Believing we are made for more extraordinary things. We try, and we work, and then we stop because, eventually, maybe we won't have to work as hard. Or remember to smile through the earthquakes of moods dropping.

Maybe one day we won't struggle, because there won't be anything to fight against; there will only be how far we've come.

Tears trickle down my face. I wipe them away and gain a smile. "So, are you excited for the big day? Only a couple of months from being Amos' official wife." When I turn, my chin rests on the edge of the bed.

"Do you ever think I make the wrong choices?" She fumbles with her fingers as she talks to me.

"Never."

"I'm serious, Z."

"I've never been more serious, Harper. You always make the right choices, even if they're hard. When you moved out—"

"Zailey, you know I didn't do that to hurt you."

All I do is give her a small smile.

"When you decided to move out, it was the right choice. I lean on you for a lot of support. It wasn't fair, especially with what you were going through too."

"We needed to grow, it was the only way."

"Like I said, you make the right choices, even if I don't know. Harper, I look up to you, and I know I am a bitch. But thank you for living this life alongside me. Thank you for not giving up on yourself, making me press on to not give up on myself either."

"Oh, Z..." Harper gets off the bed and slouches down next to me.

We sit there, side by side.

Cradling each other, holding hands like we were going to make it.

"We'll be okay, Zailey. You and I, we're going to make it out victorious. Even if we have to stay up all night just to see the sunrise. A break from the darkness, remember it will always rise."

We sit in dress pressed outfits in the front row. River to my left, and Olallie to my right, along with Lawson.

My eyes swept down the faces. River's brothers and Amos' family gathers.

She comes down the aisle, and the world stops. Harper moves slow, with uncertainty in her eyes. Amos tries to step down from the altar to go to her. But I raise a hand at him and go to her.

"I'm not going to survive, Stormy. I can feel it. I can't hurt him that way."

We both turn to look down the walkway and see his eyes pinched with concern.

"Tell me to do it, and I will. I will walk down there and marry him. But you have to promise that after I'm gone, you'll save him from blaming himself. Please, I've loved him more than I could ever love an ounce of myself." Her grip on the flowers begins to snap the stems.

"Promise me." Her voice is so silent that I barely hear the whisper.

"Never." I stare at her, fully dressed in white. Looking as uncomfortable as I feel parading to be a grown-up.

"Z, I'm serious. This is ridiculous; it might be a month, and I stop fighting. We don't know when it could be, years even." My sweet best friend who has gotten me through every imaginable crisis, has fear seeping out of her eyes.

"Look at me, Harper. If all we have are these small seconds that tick by, waiting for the inevitable, what a waste when we could be living. When the heavens decide to swallow both our souls, remember I'll be by your side. But right now, we make a choice to take one step in front of the other. Because it's not time to let go."

"Walk me down?" She opens her elbow, and I swoop in to save the day.

"Harper, if anyone deserves to live, it's you. Everyone here would line up to give you a chance at another day. I'd be first in line; Amos can kiss my ass." I give her a wink, and she lets out a good-hearted laugh.

Her doubting spell broken.

"I promise now until forever." Amos repeats it, and Harp stares at me before saying it back to him.

"We're next." River's fingers are cautious as they open, waiting for me to make a move.

My eyes go back to the altar as the bride and groom kiss. The decision is made; I choose to spend my life in love. Stop resisting and live with purpose.

So, I pick up my hand, place it in his, look deep in his eyes, and choose him.

"One day, we will be." My head leans to the side, on his shoulder. Finally, giving in to the good, the want of love, the need to heal.

THE END

And abracadabra, you are an asshole.

About the Books

This book was an emotional confession about first loves being the hardest to get over. We remember them the most, hoping they last forever.

Broken hearts are troublesome to fix.

I hope this story gives you hope, doesn't hinder your belief that miracles can happen and aren't meant to be celebrated.

Your life is valuable, and I am so glad you are alive, going through this journey with my characters and me.

The best compliment someone can receive.

Thank you for being here, reading these words.

You. Are. Not. Alone.

National Suicide Hotline:
1-800-273-8255

Follow & Connect

Facebook:

www.facebook.com/laikynmeng

Goodreads:

https://www.goodreads.com/laikynmeng

Instagram:

https://www.instagram.com/laikynmeng/

Newsletter:

http://eepurl.com/gSNiQ9

Pinterest:

https://www.pinterest.com/laikynmeng/

Website:

http://www.laikynmeng.com

About Author

Laikyn Meng is a Japanese American indie author.

She has penned over thirty publications. She maintains a steady stream of romantic expression involving diverse character representation.

She is the author of noteworthy series, the female empowered; Femme Fatale, and the family drama; Mum's the Word. Her poetry and memoirs have appeared in literary magazines.

Laikyn's unique tone is an iconic symbol for her stories.

Originally from Idaho, she resides wherever the road takes her and her three children.

Also By Laikyn Meng

FEMME FATALE SERIES

MUM'S THE WORD SERIES

SOLO MOTHERHOOD SERIES

TRUE LIES SERIES